Alan Whi

STUMBLING ON MELONS

by the same author

Crumbs Under the Skin
Half the Gladness

Carol Bruggen

STUMBLING ON MELONS

ANDRE DEUTSCH

First published in Great Britain in 1986 by
André Deutsch Limited
105 Great Russell Street, London WC1B 3LJ

British Library Cataloguing in Publication Data
Bruggen, Carol
Stumbling on melons.
I. Title
823'.914[F] PR6052.R7/
ISBN 0 233 97873 9

Phototypeset by Falcon Graphic Art Ltd
Wallington, Surrey
Printed in Great Britain by
Ebenezer Baylis and Son Ltd, Worcester

To the memory of my friend Winnie Phillips
from whom I learned all I know about loyalty, endurance,
and the art of enjoying one day at a time.

Stumbling on melons, as I pass,
Ensnared with flowers, I fall on grass.

by Andrew Marvell
from *The Garden*

1

Hector smiled at the young woman.

"So tell me about it," he invited her.

There were three chairs in his office. One stood against the far wall. One stood close to his desk, but on the other side of it. The third, a large comfortable chair, sat beside his own chair, on his side of the desk.

If his patient sat in the far chair he knew that he had a long way to go. If his patient sat in the chair which was on the other side of his desk he knew that part of his work was already complete. If his patient sat in the chair which was comfortably situated next to his own he knew that he had achieved something, but must look out for himself.

Susannah Redfern was scarcely sitting at all, simply perched, fragile as a frosted blade of grass, on the very edge of the far chair.

"There's nothing to tell," she said.

Hector fiddled with his glasses and wrote a word in the young woman's file.

Susannah stared at him. He was patronising her, of course.

"Everything begins with nothing." Hector addressed the remark to the right lens of his spectacles, breathing on it and polishing it with the sleeve of the jacket which Judith had bought him for his birthday.

It was a nice jacket, tweedy and soft. A mixture of blues and greens, it appeared neither blue nor green but something indescribable, as electrifying as the expression in his neither blue nor green eyes.

Judith was especially good about colour. She was sensitive to its moods, chose colours which both calmed and stimulated. Their flat was a constant wonder to him. Almost every day it seemed to have a new pool of colour added, a new corner brought from insignificance, as the new leaves bring meaning to the bleak branches of beech trees.

He replaced his spectacles upon his nose and examined Susannah.

Susannah stared back at him with hatred.

Why must he look at her like that? No doubt he was undressing her in his mind. Men were all the same. It didn't matter how much education they had, or how clever they were supposed to be, basically they had only one motive.

The hatred filled her up as a wave rushes into a crevice in the rocks, foaming and threshing and threatening.

If she wanted to she could dive into that torrent and never be seen again. If she allowed herself one second's indecision on the spray-dampened seaweed she would slip into it without having to make any decision.

She would be gone. It would be over.

Hector thought about Judith as he waited for his patient to decide whether she wanted to be helped up on to the beach.

They had been looking for a house. It didn't matter much to him. Wherever Judith was would be home. But she would like to have a little garden. A garden would extend the parameters of her family, though he sometimes felt as if Judith's family, extending as it did through the endless vistas of her fantasy, was large enough already.

After all, as his patient she had introduced him to an imaginary husband, Murphy, and half a dozen imaginary children who were, in fact, projections of her brothers and sisters, to say nothing of parents and aunts who could not possibly have been, in reality, as bizarre as they had become in her mind.

In real terms, they were expecting a visit from Judith's niece, Helen, who was a journalist in Adelaide. Helen had written to Judith to say that she was pregnant and intended to come to England to have the baby in July, anxious as she was not to become prominent, literally or figuratively, in her own gossip column. What she would do after that she had not decided.

3

This news had given Judith any impetus she might have needed towards nest-building. They must find a nice house with a little garden so that Helen would have somewhere to spend the last weeks of her pregnancy and bring the new baby home to.

"You can't do anything, anyway. Nobody can do anything. There's no point in me telling you. There's no point in telling anybody. There's nothing to tell. I'm nobody. I'm nothing. I don't exist. None of us exists. Even you're only a figment of my imagination. Nothing's real. People just suck you in and blow you out like a bloody whale swallowing the drowned. The world's an underwater grave. I hate it. I hate everybody. I hate you. You're just like the rest of them. Head shrinks are the worst of all. Head shrinks just float around prodding the carcases. They do it for kicks. I've got nothing to say to you. Nothing," said Hector's patient.

Hector lit the pipe he had found under the refrigerator when Judith had first taken over the organisation of his existence. He turned the match slowly round and round, watching its end blacken and curl, watching its white stem grow smaller until the flame reached his fingers and he had to drop it into the ashtray. He puffed, several short, sharp puffs to get the tobacco burning then held the bowl of the pipe and tapped its mouthpiece against his front teeth.

"Uh-huh," he replied.

2

"Right," said Pat. "Stir yourself and we'll look in the paper."

Now that she worked in Ostle Judith took the bus on Friday and joined her two old friends for lunch when they had finished the morning's work in the clothing factory.

"A house for Judith and her Hector. That's got to be something special." Pat licked her thumb and turned over the pages of the local paper.

"Mansion, I suppose," Gill added, "mansion with gold-plated taps and a French toilet with a fountain that goes up your arse-hole."

"How do you fancy a derelict barn?" asked Pat. "There's one here going for only forty thousand. Two acres of land."

"We could build a pen and keep James Holden in it. Get him away from his foreparts," suggested Gill. "We could charge to look at him. Weekends we'd be crowded out." She ate her cheese sandwich with a look of distaste, like a cat avoiding the innards of a shrew which it had slaughtered in the mistaken belief that it was a mouse.

James Holden, beloved of his workers in the factory he managed, precious to them as a source of innocent merriment and affectionately despised for his handsome appearance and ruthless efficiency, as well as for his tendency to refer to the fronts of coats as 'foreparts', would have disintegrated like a piece of cake left too long in the sun if he had ever become aware of the various fates imagined by them as being suitable for him.

"Talk sense, you dozy sod," Pat remonstrated. "We'd have to feed him."

"He could have this butty." Gill peered into her lunch. "Sodden. I'll be farting like a buffalo. Ron will be going on about the ventilation. Always blames me, even when it's the bloody cat."

Judith was looking over Pat's shoulder.

Hector, darling Hector. Judith's imagination struggled to embrace her husband as a rickety wooden fence struggles to embrace a flower-wild, mysterious garden.

We're going to have a house, like everyone else.

"That looks good," she said suddenly.

"Compact three-bedroomed dwelling with garden front and rear. Sitting room, living kitchen, three-piece bathroom suite. Gas central heating. Quiet residential area," Pat read aloud.

" 'Quiet residential area' sounds all right," Gill observed. "Round our way they get tanked up on a Saturday night then piss through your letterbox on their way home from the pub. Drives me Mam wild. My Ted says if he ever catches one of them at it he'll swing for him."

"You want to get a letterbox with a really good spring." Pat was enraged. "The dirty buggers. Worse than animals. I'd do it myself. Stand behind the front door and snap it closed on them as they got started. Cut off their ardour, that would." She made an indignant humphing sound, incredulously angry like a hamster which finds that its nest has been vandalised.

"Hector could use one of the bedrooms as a study. And the spare one would be for Helen and her baby. We don't want anything bigger than that." Judith read the advertisement again.

"You'd think they could pay a visit before last orders," Gill continued. "It's not as if they were tramping off through the Sahara."

"Men get a lot of enjoyment from it," said Judith unexpectedly. "Murphy . . . I mean my father . . ." She hesitated. Even now, she sometimes had a moment's confusion about Murphy. She knew, she knew perfectly well, that Murphy did not exist, that she had invented him and that he was composed of elements of her father, Cecil, and elements which she had created herself in order to provide herself with a companion who would suit her during the many years when she had lived a lonely, solitary life. She knew now, living with the solid reality of Hector, a real man, her real husband, that Murphy did not exist. Yet still, occasionally, she had to pause in a narrative about his exploits to remind herself of this fact. "My father," she said firmly. "I was once looking out of the bedroom window when I was drawing the curtains. We lived in the country, you know. It was a summer evening. The light was beginning to go. The leaves on the silver birch were all shivering as if they were excited. I could smell the roses and the hay. Everything was opening, bursting open with a little pop of surprise.

I noticed a figure standing quite still under the trees. It was . . . Father. I felt very moved, thinking of him communicating with the transcendental, gazing across the hillside over the fields at the dusky landscape.

Then I realised that he was tranquilly peeing into his compost heap."

Pat and Gill stared at Judith.

You never knew what was going on in Judith's mind. She said such peculiar things.

Gill was thoughtful.

"Waste not, want not," she mused.

"Well, anyway," said Pat. "About this house. Would you like us to come with you to look at it? Or will you be going with your Hector?"

"We could go and have a look first. He doesn't have a lot of time. Then if it's all right I could take him."

"Saturday morning. Tomorrow. Get your finger out in the morning, Gill. We'll meet at the bus station at half past ten." Pat enjoyed nothing as much as putting events and people in order. "We'll visit the Estate Agents and then view the prospective Jones establishment."

Judith remembered the first Saturday morning outing she had shared with Pat and Gill. They had bought a dress for her to wear at the reunion party. Her brothers and sisters and nieces and nephews had come from all over the world and met in London. That had been two years ago. She still wore the dress sometimes when she and Hector were in a romantic mood. It had been the first of many Saturday morning outings with Pat and Gill. She could no longer remember the days when she had been afraid of the town, afraid of all those amiable, disconsolate, ugly, magnificent people.

We're going to find a house for Hector and Helen and Helen's baby. Hector likes to sleep on Saturday mornings if he isn't on call. It'll be a secret about the house. I'll tell him that we're going shopping.

"And when that baby comes, don't get landed with it," Pat called after her as she went to catch her bus back to work at Ostle. "You're too old for that sort of thing, and daft enough to do it."

July. In July there will be another baby to look after. And Helen. And young Helen.

Judith looked at the sky. It was filled with rejuvenated clouds, plodding but jubilant.

"See you in the morning. And mind you don't overdo it tonight. We know what you're like, you young brides." Gill tripped over the corner of the pavement and adjusted her long legs and her feet which always appeared to be the thin flattened ends of her long legs, as if somebody had bent her and run over them with a roller.

Pat took Gill by the arm and steered her towards the factory between the rows of blackened houses and shops which hovered along the roadside like Italian peasant ladies watching the world go by.

Gill looked over her shoulder at the paving stone on which she had caught her foot.

"I must have that moved before next Friday," she announced.

Climbing on to her bus Judith thought about Hector.

Darling Hector. He'll be able to sit in the sun in the little garden and rest his poor mind.

3

The subject of her concern climbed the stairs up to the flat. He had admitted the young woman for electrotherapy treatment and would be keeping an eye on her.

He thought about her anxious hands, their nails bitten until they bled, restlessly making and unmaking fists, moving through her long hair, searching for something to hold in her shoulder bag, gripping each other, white with tension like the pale faces of hungry children.

He thought about her rage. She had kicked him when he told her that in his opinion she should come into hospital for a short course of treatment. He rubbed his shin. He wasn't sure about the electrotherapy. She was certainly very depressed. But she was also very angry.

As he reached the top of the stairs he smelled one of Judith's mixtures. Onions and peppers and aubergines, probably chicken and mushrooms too.

Good. That would help him to think. Tomorrow was Saturday. He would sleep in the morning. Then he would go across to the ward, though he wasn't on duty.

He'd just have a quiet look at Susannah when she wasn't expecting him.

4

The pageantry of the bus station on Saturday morning enthralled Judith. Small men carried large suitcases. Ample women carried exiguous babies. Medium-sized boys carried massive knapsacks. Girls with plenty to cover covered very little of it and carried themselves as if they knew that the cinema audience of the world held its breath in admiration. Children dropped their ice-lollies and stood stunned, staring at the wreckage. Dad shouted, asserting himself.

"Don't let him see you doing that," whispered Mum.

Arrivals and departures took place between the metal barriers which separated the different bus queues as if the casual,

"See you,"

of the lovers leaving each other for ever to return to the inadequate familiarity of their former existence, and the tumultuous,

"Welcome home son,"

of the father who had not thought the lad would survive a whole term, and the querulous,

"Don't leave it so long, next time,"

of the frail elderly monster whose children paid their dutiful visits and escaped her maternal custody with the joyful swoop of a swallow departing for more clement climes, boarding the bus home to Bradford: as if all these were somehow transformed by their transition through the ugly cement structure of the bus station itself, from mundane to mystical events, as the wafer and the wine are changed to flesh and blood.

Aunts and uncles, friends, grandchildren, the tottery old, the lonely young were on the move, making pilgrimages to

Manchester, Blackpool, Preston, Clitheroe, Slaidburn, even to that distant unknown shrine, London, whence they would return festooned with parcels and radiant with the sorcerous dust of brief encounters.

"You dozy bugger, we're over here," shouted Gill from under the clock. "We've been standing here for ten minutes. Time's valuable to folks like us, you know. Time's money. Not much, but money. Where the hell have you been?"

Judith, bright red and conscious of the drama shifting from the stage to the auditorium as the actors forgot their parts momentarily and watched her hurrying to her rendezvous before her friend could disclose the rest of the plot, called back confusedly,

"Sorry. I'm coming."

"Late for everything, our Judith. Even though she's wed, you'll notice, she still turns up late for appointments. What was it today? Your Hector felt randy when it was time to get up? We've been watching the hours go by. Can't help noticing the time, you know, standing here like cheese at fourpence under a sodding clock." Gill puffed at her cigarette and wafted the smoke away from her eyes with an elegant hand.

Judith wondered, as always, how Gill knew what she had been doing.

Hector had, indeed, woken when she was getting quietly out of bed and drawn her sleepily back beside him. She could still feel the warmth of his solid chest, his arms which enclosed her as the evening light encloses a round trembling moon amongst the trees on the hill, his hands, in which she had first recognised herself, giving authority to every cell for a celebration, a jubilee, a coronation of the senses, his flesh against and within her thin body drawing from her such a sunset of sexuality that she became, like the moon in the trees, a high embodiment of forces beyond reckoning.

"She's blushing. Having a hot flush, I expect." Gill realised without embarrassment that she'd accidentally rung the bell.

"No taste, my pal. Close your mouth or hold your tongue, Gill." Pat tried to draw together the threads of the morning, straggling off into disorder and chaos as they appeared to be. "You're always opening your mouth and putting your foot in it. It's a warm morning, that's all. Pay no attention to her, Judith. Now come on, the pair of you. I've rung up and they'll let us have the key. By the time we arrive the bloody house will have been sold and the new occupants moved in." She steered them towards the estate agent's premises.

Really, you couldn't get any sense out of either of them, one all gas and air, the other sweating like a lovesick calf.

5

Susannah sat on her hands. She was very conscious of her hands. For the whole of her twenty-six years she had tried not to bite her fingernails. Her hands were like a livid birthmark, something she wanted to hide, something that appalled her, something that set her apart from other people. But unlike a birthmark they were her own fault. All she had to do was stop biting their torn painful nails.

Sometimes as a child she had dreamed about having long, painted nails, red ones. She had thought that this would make her like other girls, and later she had thought that it would make her like other women. Her father had thrashed her for biting her nails. She had wanted to please her father, when she was small. She had done everything she could to please him. He had never been pleased. She had wanted to be beautiful to please her father. If she had beautiful nails she would be beautiful.

An Asian girl sat silently staring at the pattern on the curtains of the day-room.

Susannah approached her.

"Electrotherapy," she said, "what's electrotherapy like?"

The Asian girl didn't respond. Since yesterday afternoon when she had been admitted and first noticed the Asian girl sitting by herself Susannah had not heard her say a word. The Asian girl spoke to nobody.

"Is it terrible?" Susannah persisted.

The Asian girl had hands which rested silently, one upon the other, speechless, uncommunicative hands, a pale ochre colour with neat, white, shining nails.

"I'm speaking to you," said Susannah.

The Asian girl didn't respond.

"Oh, please yourself."

The Asian girl raised her head and looked at Susannah with eyes black and guarded as a starless night.

"At least you're not deaf. And you don't bite your bloody nails." Susannah stood up and began to pace around the day-room.

"Why don't you find something to do, my dear?" Nurse Ramsden asked. Nurse Ramsden was small, like a woodland animal. She moved swiftly and purposefully in this desert, as though constantly pursuing and endeavouring to prevent the escape of optimism.

"I'm not your dear," Susannah replied.

"If you do something the time will go more quickly," said Nurse Ramsden.

"Like bloody what?" demanded Susannah. "Like what do you expect me to do in this morgue? Look at them all. Look at the vegetables. Rows of cabbages in a cabbage patch. Knitting squares, knitting scarves, knitting sweaters for people they can't remember. Knitting their guts into shapeless bundles. Knitting makes me puke."

"You could do something else," said Nurse Ramsden. "There are some good jigsaws in the cupboard."

"Jigsaws make me puke."

"Is there anything that doesn't make you puke? I'll make you a cup of tea if you're thirsty."

"I don't like tea."

"How about a game of cards? Tessa over there is always looking for somebody to play cards with." Nurse Ramsden indicated a tired-looking woman with long grey hair who was patiently dealing out two hands of tattered playing cards although she was quite alone.

"She looks as if she needed a game of Russian roulette," said Susannah.

"Sometimes if you try to help somebody else it makes you feel better," Nurse Ramsden explained, watching regretfully as the hope she had been following made for the fire escape.

6

Hector did not remain asleep for the whole morning. Wandering into the kitchen to make himself some breakfast he found a note from Judith.

"Darling, I've gone shopping with Gill and Pat. What a nice beginning for a nice day."

He remembered. She was right. It had been a nice beginning.

He made himself some toast.

He felt like a king.

In the years after his first wife had left him he had become so used to the tumult of disturbed emotions, both in himself and in his patients, that his standard of happiness had dropped like flags at half-mast, in mourning for humankind. Now he was certain that for every poor creature he saw in despair there could be not just better things, but much better things.

He drank his coffee and looked at his watch. It was eleven o'clock.

Into his mind, like a solitary cloud in a bright sky, floated Susannah. She would be having her first treatment on Monday. Unless he managed to waft her into a more formative frame of mind there would be trouble. One protesting patient could upset the whole session.

Judith wouldn't be back for another hour. He wouldn't wait until this afternoon. He would go across to the hospital now.

7

Susannah had left the knitters. She was sitting on one of the sofas kept for visitors in a corridor with a fish tank at the end of it.

Wearing a yellow aertex shirt and pale brown jeans to create an atmosphere of casual encounter Hector strolled along the corridor and sat down beside her.

"Oh, the big shrink. I didn't know they shrank on Saturdays." Susannah greeted him with a smile which would have filled the heart of a cobra with an icy sensation. She edged away from him.

She was wearing a T-shirt with the words 'I am a virgin' written on it in large letters which wandered up and down across her meagre bosom, and a faded cotton skirt with a pocket which had come unstitched down one side.

"Just called in to say hello." Hector struck a match and applied it to his pipe, hoping to observe her through its fumes, if he could persuade it to fume. He struck another match, and another.

"Try some magic. You can perform miracles, can't you? Hypnotise it. Call down fire from heaven," suggested the young woman.

"Why do you chew your nails? You make them sore." Hector put the three dead matches in an ashtray which stood on one leg like a stork. He picked up Susannah's hand and examined it. Susannah snatched her hand away as if it had been bitten.

"Fuck off, shrink. Fuck off. Go and find somebody else to molest. I know all about trick cyclists. You're not going to get around me, you know. Nobody gets around me. I can take care of myself. And if you ever touch me again, or come within a hundred miles of me I shall throw myself through the nearest window. Men who are old enough to be the fathers of girls my age should leave them alone and not ask them damned silly questions and pry into their lives and play God when the whole place is falling to pieces around their ears," said Susannah.

Hector stared into the bowl of his pipe. He pressed the tobacco down gingerly with his thumb and replaced the stem in his mouth.

He puffed hard and sighed with pleasure as it began to glow.

Exhaling the smoke he addressed a large goldfish which was opening and closing its mouth at the front of the tank as if it were conversing with somebody who was deaf.

"You didn't answer my question," he replied.

8

Hector and Judith had lunch in silence. It wasn't an uncomfortable silence. It was the kind of silence which falls upon a couple when they know each other well, when they are sexually happy, and when each of them has something in mind which it feels the other need not be told about.

The house had been a dismal failure. Even Gill, whose standards of homemaking did not live up to Pat's, had dismissed it.

"Fur coats and no knickers. Wouldn't lend you a bob for the meter if your toes were dropping off. If that's a quiet residential area, give me a ghetto. Even the mice'd be at each other's throats in that place."

Pat, who liked a bit of decency and order, thought no better of it.

"Posh, but not you and Hector, love. Posh, but not real posh. If you're going to be posh, do the job properly and get a semi," she said.

Judith hadn't been as conscious of the residential area as the other two, but there had been an atmosphere about the house itself which distressed her deeply.

It was not in the stones of the actual building. It was nothing to do with the regency wallpaper which fought with the Axminster carpets which fought with the ready-made curtains from Woolworth's, all included in the price, or anything to do with the orange bathroom fittings. It was in the air. As they entered the front door she knew that in this house there had been great unhappiness.

Unhappiness is often, sometimes at the same time, sometimes much later, offset by happiness in equal proportions.

But in this house unhappiness had not been offset.

In this house there had been striving and pretension, discontent, bitterness and envy. How she knew this she could not have explained. But she knew it. These humours hung about the three bedrooms, one of which, in any case, would barely have held Hector's desk, let alone his books. They hung about the small, tight garden aching with plants which, though the house had obviously been empty for some time, were still behaving as if they were under the eye of a loveless gardener, standing forlornly in undernourished rows.

By the time they had inspected every room and returned to the front door with its stained glass she was shivering.

"Well," said Gill, surveying the front door, "for sure they wouldn't piss through your letterbox. It's too high up."

"I don't suppose they do things like that around here." Pat was subdued.

"Not at all, you mean. If they've all got orange toilets I daresay they'd prefer to keep it to themselves. Imagine looking into that the morning after. Scare the shit out of you," said Gill thoughtfully.

Remembering her twenty-five years in Mackworth Street, with the purple front door, Judith felt that these indications were not incidental. It was not a question of taste. It was not a question of education. It was not a question of the relative value of material possessions.

It was a matter of how important possessions were to their owner. In this house things which they had and things which they did not have became more important than all the disingenuous associations which crown the bleakest lives with laughter and enjoyment as a million pink petals crown the almond tree in the early summer. In this house the things had sucked the vitality out of the people. When they went, taking their acquisitions with them, they left behind a despondency which even a transfusion of Judith and Hector's happiness could not have removed.

For Judith the house was, in effect, haunted.

She wouldn't spoil Hector's lunch by telling him about it.

She glanced at his handsome face, watched his marvellous hands performing the routine ritual of eating, loved his authority, his steadfastness, her security with him.

Hector was thinking about his fierce patient. He knew something of her background, of course. He knew that her parents had separated when she was seven, that she had disliked her stepfather, that she had given birth to a child when she was sixteen. But he must hear these things from Susannah herself. Until she had confided in him he was helpless.

He became aware of Judith's silence, her eyes upon him.

Her eyes, their unquestioning adoration, released his wide smile.

"Now, what have you been up to, creeping off like that before I was properly awake?" he asked. "Was it a clandestine assignment? Something you didn't want me to know about? Some dark secret?" He filled his coffee cup, then added, "I can't be losing parts of your life, you know. You mustn't steal your morning from me."

Judith wondered why it was that everybody always knew just what she had been doing.

9

"Are you any good at crossword puzzles?" asked Nurse Ramsden, trying with infinite concern to find something which would stop Susannah's endless pacing about like a lioness in search of her cubs.

"You've got to be joking," said Susannah. "I left school before I was sixteen with no 'O' levels and nothing in my head that wouldn't have left a space in a peapod."

"Crossword puzzles are different," Nurse Ramsden explained seriously, "you don't have to be able to pass exams to do crossword puzzles. It's a gift, partly a gift and partly an awareness of words. I thought that as you seem to talk a lot you might be into crossword puzzles."

"Crossword puzzles make me puke," Susannah explained in return.

"What would you like to do, I mean if I said you could do anything you wanted to?"

"I'd have a cigarette."

"No, my dear, I wouldn't have a cigarette if I were you. Not before the anaesthetic. You'll feel sick afterwards if you do."

"I feel sick now."

"Then you'll feel sicker."

Susannah prowled to the window and looked out.

The paths leading to different hospital buildings were deserted. It was only eight o'clock in the morning but the day in the ward seemed to have been going on since the Stone Age. Beyond the clinic in which she had visited Hector's office she could see flats where some of the medical staff lived.

She watched a thin, middle-aged woman emerge from one

of these and turn, laughing, to speak to somebody who was following her.

It was her shrink.

The woman had a sheaf of white hair, bright in the morning light like a greeting. Funny, that. She didn't look old enough to have white hair. The psychiatrist was laughing, too.

Susannah watched as they drew apart, then together again, then apart. They stopped laughing and embraced, examining each other for a moment before they did so, as if they had only just met and felt that they were going to like each other. Then the psychiatrist bent and kissed the woman, very gently, as if to find out something that he had always wanted to know. The woman blushed.

For God's sake. The woman was blushing. A middle-aged woman blushing because she had been kissed by a middle-aged psychiatrist.

Susannah wondered whether they were the sort of people who had an orgasm every time they met.

The psychiatrist waved to his wife and strode cheerfully towards the hospital. His wife walked briskly away in the opposite direction.

A kind of hopeless fury seeped into Susannah's consciousness. It felt like the cold, grey water left in a thick slurry at the bottom of the mop bucket when the last traces of soap have been defeated.

"Come along now, my dear," said Nurse Ramsden, taking Susannah's arm.

"I'm not your dear. And I wish you wouldn't touch me," Susannah snarled.

"They are going to be ready for us to go up for our ECT soon so let's get ready. Bra off. Dressing gown on. Nothing else. Just dressing gown and panties. That's all we need."

"You're having it too, are you?"

Susannah's sarcasm was wasted on Nurse Ramsden.

She had heard it all before.

10

Climbing the wide staircase at the packaging firm where she had worked since she was made redundant by the garment factory Judith thought about houses.

" 'Allo, love," said Tulip. "Me bras have come. Didn't have time to try them on. Undo the parcel tonight."

Tulip loved underwear. She ran a mail order club and the room she occupied in her parents' house was overflowing with her purchases – lacy, floppy, silky, silly clothing to wear under the formal Eastern exterior.

Today the exterior consisted of a turquoise sari and white trousers, a heavily embroidered blouse with golden scrolls and her usual almost nonexistent sandals. Her long black hair was braided down the back in two plaits and the two plaits had been twisted together and fastened at the nape of her neck with a turquoise plastic bobble, making a thick rope like the tail of a shire horse dressed up for an agricultural show.

Climbing the stairs beside Judith she was panting slightly, her cheeks a deep red under the lovely brown of her skin, a diamanté jewel in the side of her nostril gleaming like a raindrop on a petal.

"Any news of the husband?" Judith asked.

Tulip's husband was a source of constant merriment. He was always just about to come to England.

"He says he'll be here by the end of the summer." Tulip giggled. She had a bit of sorting out to do in her life before then.

"You should save your new bras," Judith suggested.

"No chance. Try them on, show them off, wear them out." Tulip giggled again.

Tulip was better at running her mail order club than she was at her job in the packaging firm. In spite of her exotic, delicate appearance she was as clumsy as a labrador puppy. The tasks they performed were not paid for on a piecework basis so the women were not in a great hurry. Of course, they had to work as quickly and efficiently as possible. But Tulip was always pacing herself, trying to get more done than Hannah and Susan and Judith, trying to be the first one to move on to the next project, trying to invent new routines which would make the packaging, the labelling, the pasting, the cutting, the tying, the filling of envelopes with catalogues and compliment slips and free offers as swift a process as slipping through the front door of the building when she had clocked out. No doubt she felt that if she remained ahead in her race against time she would reach the end of the day before the others.

Because of her haphazardness and the speed at which she did things, it was always possible to distinguish Tulip's work in the piles of finished products on the sorting tables. Tulip's boxes were the ones which kept popping open as the hastily applied sellotape burst asunder. Tulip's envelopes were the ones on which the address labels had become affixed in the corner instead of in the middle, or on which the surface had been rubbed away where she had applied them upside down and had to remove and re-apply them. Tulip's free offers were the ones from which the free offer had been accidentally omitted. Tulip's table was the table on which the scissors, the sellotape, the toilet bags, and the brochures were all mixed up while she rummaged through an hour's work to find out why she had five pieces of free scented oil soap left over.

Judith loved Tulip. In spite of her apparently oriental origins Tulip was as Lancastrian as stew an' 'ard.

"Oh shit," said Tulip, surveying the supervisor's table. "It's them horrible Shinies again today. When we have to do them I can't tell me arse from me elbow."

Judith settled herself at her table and arranged the pieces of corrugated card, the bags of coins and the slips so that she was ready to swing into action. She placed her feet on the bar underneath, pressed her spine against the back of her chair and began to work methodically, sorting, sticking on, sealing in the envelopes.

The idea of the haunted house returned to her mind. Uncomfortable, tight feelings communicated to her by the house crept out of her subconscious with their tails between their legs. These feelings had no home there. She would not entertain the thought of these unhappy people in the picnic of her mind. They could live as they liked. They could run in the rat-wheel. Let them aspire and achieve and suffer.

She only wanted to be. This was her treasure, given to her by Hector. She would cherish it for him.

"Knitbone," said Hannah to the back of Susan's head. "Get a leaf of it and wrap it around her little ankle. Take out the swelling."

"It's only a bruise."

"Else get it dried and put it in water. Soak her foot in it. Cures everything. Put Mephistopheles right when he had hardpad."

"She's not a dog, you know," objected Susan, who though she was pale as a snowdrop and looked as if she might melt under the radiance of Hannah's redbrick countenance was not going to be warmed into using veterinary medicines on her beloved child.

"Dogs, kids, what the hell," said Hannah cheerfully. "Knitbone cures them all. I'll bring you a root from my garden. You can grow it in your windowbox. Isn't that so, Judith?" She turned and looked enquiringly at Judith's abstracted face.

"I really don't know." Judith shook off the spectral figures occupying that orange bathroom suite. "I haven't got a windowbox."

"Tulip," cried Mrs Eccles from the far end of the room, "what are you doing, dear?"

"Just trying to get me scissors out of this crack," Tulip replied from the floor under her table.

11

Susannah fidgeted in the queue. She was wearing a white dressing gown with pink and blue and purple flowers all over it, joined together by tiny green leaves. It had wide, frilled cuffs and bore the expensive label of a French manufacturer. Susannah had bought it at the Church of England Children's Society shop for twenty pence.

The general effect of the dressing gown was one of soft, pampered luxury. It belonged to that strata of people who have private medical care and address their consultants by their Christian names. It also gave an impression of quiet, rural peace, its pattern bright and clearly defined against the background like crocus blooms on a snowy lawn.

"Why we have to stand here like sodding cows I can't imagine," said Susannah from its genteel interior. "It's bad enough knowing that the buggers are out to finish you off without waiting for three hours in the abattoir. Why can't they just get on with it? Why are we standing here on these fucking stairs like something waiting to be born? It's enough to worry about, being electrocuted, without being made to line up with the cabbages, shitting bricks."

"The answer to your question is that like all hospitals we are understaffed and overworked and there isn't room for everyone who is going to be treated to wait upstairs and you wouldn't want to be in the ward where it was all going on, would you?" Nurse Ramsden replied, helping the grey-haired woman who was shuffling up the stairs still carrying her battered playing cards. "Now Tessa, let me keep those safely for you until afterwards. I'll have a game of gin rummy with you this afternoon," she promised.

"Don't shout at me," Susannah complained.

"I'm not shouting at you. It's just that we are busy and if you make provocative remarks the other patients, many of whom are very sick, will become frightened." Nurse Ramsden put a protective arm around Tessa.

"What about me? Don't you think I'm bloody frightened? You could be standing in it up to your knees," said Susannah.

"When it's all over I'll bring you a nice cup of tea and you won't remember anything about it."

"Tea makes me puke."

"Well, something nice. What would you like?"

Susannah fiddled with her hair. It hung down her back, free of its usual tiny plaits, sticking stiff and straight in places and crinkled like stage hair before it has been teased out in others. She spent a lot of time making the little braids in her hair. It gave her satisfaction to see how many of the plaits she could accommodate around her small head.

If Gavin had been a girl she would have plaited his hair. Gavin. He had been blond, much blonder than she was, almost like an albino, except for his critical blue eyes. His eyes had always unnerved her. From the age at which he could understand adults at all he had stared at them and worked out how they could be manipulated. He knew that his grandmother was his best bet.

But it was his mother, Susannah, who had devoted herself to him for the whole of his seven years.

Now all she could remember of that seven years was shouts of warning, the screaming fury of tyres and the high-pitched wailing of a car horn which went on and on in her mind like the horrifying howl of an animal caught in a steel trap.

Then she had seen Gavin, distorted and discoloured in a slowly spreading flower of blood.

"I'd like to be dead," said Susannah. "See if you can arrange it."

"Oh, you won't feel like that when you have had some treatment." Nurse Ramsden touched Susannah's eccentric head. "Haven't you got pretty hair?" She preferred the direct approach to patients. Sometimes a little thing made them feel better than complicated discussions.

"I'd be glad if you wouldn't lay hands on me. I don't know if you are into women, but I'm straight. And my hair is full of blood. And my head is full of blood. So piss off and have your game of gin rummy." Susannah was preparing for a long monologue but she caught sight of a tall young male nurse making his way past the patients on the stairs to reach the treatment ward.

"Are you Jonathan Miller?" she asked with interest. She had seen Jonathan Miller on the television a long time ago and liked him.

The young male nurse winked at Nurse Ramsden.

"No, love, I'm Douglas, his brother," he replied.

Susannah thought this was a good omen.

If Jonathan Miller's brother was here they couldn't mess things up too badly.

The queue shuffled patiently up the steps one at a time, making its way into the big ward.

Susannah suddenly became frantic. The woman behind her who was wearing a red dressing gown which smelled of disinfectant tottered and bumped into her.

"Shove off. Stay on your own bloody step. We're not in a hurry, you know," she shouted.

"Don't shout at me," the woman complained.

"Well, tell me why we're here, then. Tell me what the hell we are doing all standing here like this." She raised her voice and addressed the bowed, submissive backs above her on the stairs. She turned and repeated her question to the subdued, hopeless faces behind her.

"Why are we here? We're not a herd of bloody cows. Plop, plop, plop up the stairs like cows. Well, you lot can go and be milked. They're not getting me. I'm off."

There was a flutter of anxiety and slow motion panic as Susannah began to push her way down the stairs, thrusting aside the wall of expressionless female bodies and heading for the door of the ward. Without wondering what she was doing the women began to follow her, trailing obediently along in her wake as corks follow the current of a river.

Before Nurse Ramsden could stem the tide it had flowed

docilely out into the hospital grounds, the patients plodding in their dressing gowns and downtrodden bedroom slippers in twos and threes towards the main gate.

"Oh hell," muttered Nurse Ramsden, leaving Tessa who stood where she was halfway up the stairs, alone.

"Nurse," called Tessa as Nurse Ramsden ran to find the male nurses from the treatment ward, "Nurse, can I have me cards back?"

Visitors to the hospital were surprised to see the patients, led by a Valkyrie in a flowered dressing gown who was running as fast as the flapping folds of this garment would allow, walking sedately and sedatedly out of the hospital.

"Probably another bomb scare," said the porter Fred to his mate Eric who was mending the light fuse.

"Must have gone off, judging by yon at front," Eric mused, and they both chuckled appreciatively as the stream of women passed the porter's lodge and trickled comfortably in amongst the flood of pedestrians outside.

Susannah had not decided where she would go. She only knew that if she had reached the top of those stairs she would have died.

Four male nurses had arrived, panting, outside the gates and were deftly extricating the patients from the passers-by, many of whom wore the same expression of uncurious toleration as the patients themselves.

Pausing before she crossed the road Susannah heard shouts. Douglas Miller and a nurse with a flowing red beard, their white uniforms gleaming in the sunshine, were after her. Their long legs absorbed the distance faster than Susannah's legs, soaking up the space as the legs of insects soak up the distance on the top of a pool.

As she was halfway across the road a car speeding from her right braked urgently and slid sideways across the tarmac, coming to rest with a splintering, metallic uproar against a small van which had been minding its own business trundling down the opposite side of the road.

As the occupants of these two vehicles disembarked and began to argue about how the accident had occurred they were assisted by the varying accounts of the twenty or thirty people at the scene, who had begun to appreciate that something out of the usual run of things was happening.

Susannah, on the far pavement, setting off up the hill towards some unknown destination, suddenly felt herself being raised from the ground.

Douglas Miller held her firmly by one elbow and his bearded colleague held her even more firmly by the other.

Impeded by the glamorous dressing gown she continued to make running movements but her feet were several inches above the pavement.

The two nurses kept Susannah suspended lightly between them as they propelled her, her legs still churning, back across the road which was now blocked by cars. Like a distraught bee held captive in a spider's web, Susannah was transported past the crowd of jolly pedestrians.

A small cheerful woman wearing a pinny emerged from a house by the bus stop and began to sweep up the broken glass which littered the road, as if this had merely been an extension of her front hallway.

"Come in threes, you know. Dog broke its leg this morning. There's another to happen before the day's over."

Seeing that she could not avoid being carried back through the gates to the execution line Susannah drew together the edges of her dignity and her dressing gown, disarranged as they had become.

"Gentlemen," she said in a small voice, "gentlemen, no violence, please."

The despair which rolled across the skies of her mind was thick and black and ominous as thunder.

She hoped she would die. She had suffered enough. She didn't want to wake up.

But as she was restored to the ground and trotted for a few uncertain steps between the two big male nurses, still held firmly by her elbows, she caught a glimpse of Hector, talking to one of the restored women as she slopped back up the steps. A little movement, no more than the fluttering of an eyelash, half mischievous, half desperate, stirred her psyche.

"OK. You can let go now," she said. "I'll come quietly. What the hell. Makes no bloody odds. Win some, lose some. Who cares? Certainly not you. Not me. Why worry? You can only die once. Beats knitting. I'd rather die threshing about like a butterfly under a pin than knitting. A moment of glory. Susannah's moment of glory. The way out. You're going to kill me, aren't you?"

The two nurses released her elbows and relaxed.

"No love," said Douglas Miller soberly, "we're not allowed to do that."

12

Hector himself was to plunge the anaesthetic needle into the vein of Susannah's left arm.

She had ceased to struggle. She had acquiesced. She had submitted to the routine – the routine, ritual indignity which accompanied the administering of ECT. She had become one of the uncomplaining cows.

She lay on one of the stripped beds in the large ward which had been prepared for the electrotherapy session. The sleeve of her garden dressing gown had been rolled back to expose the big vein. Her eyes were closed as she proffered herself to the executioners.

Hector felt an inexplicable sense of panic.

Here was somebody whom they had reduced from an uncontrollable force to a sacrificial victim. She had given up her fight as a young horse, realising that it cannot unseat its rider, ceases to rear and stampede and crash against the wooden railings and trots submissively about the enclosure.

Using ECT was always a gamble. They had changed behaviour patterns. They had in some cases destroyed a final, vital flicker of existence. Occasionally they had lost a life altogether.

What was he responsible for doing to this young woman? He glanced at the shapeless bodies humped on the beds beyond hers. They were like old logs, saturated by the afflictions of their lives, sinking lower and lower until they rested on the mud of the river bed to wait for the day when the water would be gone.

What he was about to inflict on her might improve Susannah's attitude and reduce her suffering.

Or it might increase it enormously.

Or it might kill her.

Making conversational flutterings it occurred to him that this moment might be a link between chaos and order. Or it might merely signal the end of another human conflict, the final going through into another room, if there was another room, the conclusion of a lifetime's striving and failure. It might set her on a new course. Or it might end her journey as effectively as one would end the journey of a small black beetle by stepping on it.

"Well, Susannah," he said cheerfully, "I see you've given me a beautiful vein. It's a pleasure to find a vein like that. Some of them won't come anywhere near the surface." He hoped his voice wasn't giving away the doubt he was feeling.

After all, lying there with her skimpy figure and ridiculous hair, her torn, damaged nails and look of apprehensive submission she was alive, and she was rational.

Was he doing the right thing? Was he going to turn her into an obsessive solitary like old Tessa, a total vacancy like the Asian girl, even an automated knitting machine like most of the women, without ideas, without the ordinary motives of ordinary living?

What was he about to do to her?

What were his own motives?

The sweat shone across his forehead like the glitter on a frozen lawn.

Susannah looked up at him, opening her eyes to see why the needle had not yet been inserted.

Whatever happened, one way or the other, it didn't matter. She was reconciled.

With a shock she realised that Hector was in a panic.

"For God's sake," she said, "get on with it. I'm not worth worrying about. You're doing it all the time. I'm just like the others. What do I have to do, beg on my knees? I thought you witch doctors knew all the answers. Surely you're not going to change your mind now. It either works or it doesn't work. What the hell." She closed her eyes again and turned her head away.

Hector's hand was shaking.

He remembered Judith's first ECT session. Her wrists were still bandaged after her assault upon herself with the broken light bulb. She had been in a state of profound depression, confused, deluded, withdrawn. Much worse than Susannah. For many months after that first session there had been uphill, thankless toil. But look what it had begun.

Seeing Judith lying with her arm stretched out, the bandages tight around her wrists, he had not seen in her the serene person that she had become. He had certainly not anticipated that she would become his wife.

He inserted the needle deftly into Susannah's raised vein and put an end to her years of enragement.

As she felt the prick of the needle Susannah experienced a sense of icy numbness. It was happening. She had given her consent. She had told them to destroy her. They were destroying her.

To say that she was not afraid would be misleading.

She was afraid. She was terrified.

But she was also excited. She knew that she had given something to Hector. It was a long time since she had given anything to anybody. After the death of her child she had taken, viciously, taken with greed and hatred, taken trust and torn it into little pieces, taken goodwill and transformed it into terror, taken kindness and made it appear weakness and folly. She had taken from everybody. But most of all she had taken from men. From all the men with whom she had lived after Gavin was killed she had taken their masculinity, their self-respect, their sexuality. Why not? What had a man ever done for her?

Now, for the first time since the child's death she had given something.

She had given resolution to Hector when he was in doubt. And she had given it to him in response to his kindness, enlarging instead of diminishing both him and herself.

In the fragment of time between the prick of the needle and the jerk of her head sideways she felt a kind of well-being that she hadn't known in her twenty-six years. It was warm and colourful and musical, it was full of peace and harmony. The cold water of the mop bucket had been replaced by very hot, clean, clear water, its bubbles parading themselves richly on the surface. It was a better feeling than the feeling induced by alcohol, by drugs, by cruelty.

As she crashed through a barrier of sensual splendour into oblivion a word formed in her mind. Dropping like a swallow from a brilliant sky she heard herself say,

"Heck."

Then she was gone.

Douglas Miller fixed the electrodes to her temples. The doctors made their way along the crowded aisles encouraging the patients and preparing them for their uncertain conversion.

13

During the evening there was a thunderstorm.

"Better switch the television off," Judith said. The screen was like a lake drawn in every direction by the wind, ruffled and spiked and writhing.

"Not a good picture," Hector agreed.

"Not that. The electricity," Judith explained.

"What's the electricity doing?" Hector asked.

"It's going rampant."

Hector had not been able to stay and watch over Susannah. He had once seen a young patient die while having electrotherapy.

"Rampant?" he said.

"Rampant." Judith was firm. "It gets into everything, you know. It comes out of the clouds and takes over. Once it gets hold there's no stopping it. Inside that television set every molecule could be alive and we wouldn't know anything about it until it got us. You can't tell from the outside. Just a shadowy shape, a tingling, and that's us gone."

"You've had experience of this sort of thing?" Hector lit his pipe.

"Sarah used to tell us about it."

"Sarah was up on electricity?" Hector tried to disengage the concept of an eccentric mother-in-law whom he had never met from the concept of a ward filled with patients whose bodies were being reduced to frenetic caricatures of themselves by the application of electrical impulses to the brain.

"Well, you know. She thought it would come out of the taps and mingle with the drinking water."

"Just during storms?" Hector wondered what had happened to Susannah during the rest of the morning.

"And when the immersion heater was on. She thought it was very dangerous putting the two things together."

Hector switched the television off and settled himself comfortably on the rambling sofa. Judith lay down beside him and he drew her against him.

"She terrified the children." Judith could feel Hector's chin resting on the top of her head. She knew that if she kept on talking he wouldn't move. This situation was a continuous connective, a binding that encircled the whole of the time they had known each other as a piece of braid encircles a skirt with pattern and colour. "Mind you, Father terrified the children, too. Once Fred and Stephen climbed out of the bedroom window on to the roof of the shed."

"Only once," murmured Hector, trying to smoke his pipe without setting fire to his wife's hair and only partially succeeding.

"Well, more than once. But that's not the story."

"Tell me the story." Hector sat up and began to beat all around himself in a vain attempt to locate and extinguish a stray particle of smouldering tobacco whose whereabouts he suddenly couldn't account for. He beat about Judith's shoulders and felt her hair, searching for signs of combustion.

Deprived of the joys of storytelling during his own antiseptic childhood, ever since Judith, as his patient, had begun to reveal her imagination to him, these interludes had been his chief delight. He did not want to mar this one by setting them both on fire.

"I'd tell you the story if I knew what you were doing." Judith was aware that the talking routine wouldn't keep him still and close to her if he had something else on his mind.

"No, no. It's all right. Just that we're burning," Hector said absently, finding the fire, trapping it in his handkerchief and putting it carefully into his glasses case, thinking that the lack of oxygen there would extinguish it. "Go on." He settled himself again.

"They took the ladder from the bunk beds and walked about for a bit. Then Stephen climbed back up the ladder and pulled it inside the bedroom, leaving Fred on the roof. They were very small. About four.

'Stephen,' said Fred, 'I think I'll come back in now.'

Stephen lowered the laundry basket, which fell on top of Fred.

'Turn it upside down and stand on it. You'll be able to climb back in,' he advised.

Fred turned the laundry basket over and stood on it. He reached up. The tips of his fingers barely touched the bottom of the windowsill.

'I can't do it,' he said in a practical way, trying to gauge Stephen's mood. Stephen looked down at Fred and smiled.

While I was trying to decide what to do, not wanting to alarm Fred, I heard Father's voice in the bedroom.

'What the bloody hell's going on here?' he enquired in his usual calm, reasonable manner. Stephen disappeared like a rabbit down a hole.

I could see Fred trembling on the roof. He didn't seem to be able to move, standing quite still on the laundry basket with his fingers held as if by magnetism to the bottom of the windowsill.

Father looked out of the window.

'And you,' he thundered, 'you can stay out there all night.' He slammed the window closed and went off in search of Stephen. By the time I rescued Fred his face was the colour of the underside of birch leaves."

"It's people like Cecil who provide me with my livelihood," Hector observed, opening his glasses case and noting with scientific satisfaction that the fire had gone out.

"There wasn't really any need for it, but he nailed the window closed, making the twins hold the nails for him," Judith concluded. She could feel Hector's stomach against her back, his hands quiet now. She hoped he might fall asleep. It was lovely when he fell asleep in the evening. It made her feel useful.

Judith thought that she could not be happier. Being with Hector like this was like wandering up and down amongst rows and rows of hollyhocks in an overgrown garden. This garden was the years in which she had brought up her six brothers and sisters in the chaotic household of her mother Sarah and her father Cecil. These years had driven her to despair. In living them again with Hector as his patient she had discovered that what she had thought to be intolerable had in fact been herself. In living them again she had come to accept what the rest of the world accepted as reality. She had also provided Hector accidentally with what he now possessed.

Hector polished his spectacles on the corner of Judith's sweater.

He was wondering about Susannah.

"Of course," said Judith, "they still went out on the roof. But they had to climb up from below."

14

There was nothing. There was nothing at all, anywhere.

They sat in silence.

Nurse Ramsden handed them cups of tea.

"Now then, you see, it was nothing," she said.

She was right. It had been nothing. There was nothing. Nothing at all.

A young woman in a white dressing gown covered with pink and mauve and blue flowers drank a cup of tea, awkwardly, as if she had never drunk a cup of tea before.

It did not make her puke.

She didn't know who she was. She didn't particularly notice that she didn't know who she was. It didn't worry her at all. Nothing worried her. She didn't feel worried. She didn't feel anything.

Like a small metal robot she stood up and walked stiffly to the kitchen with her empty cup. How she knew where the ward kitchen was she couldn't have explained. It all looked familiar to her, yet she didn't know that she had ever been there before.

She rinsed her cup under the tap and placed it on the stainless steel draining board. She rinsed her saucer and leaned it against her cup. Then she took a damp, striped cotton tea towel from the rail and tried to dry the cup and saucer. Because the tea towel was damp it didn't absorb the water. She wiped the cup and saucer again with the damp tea towel. Then she wiped them again. She wiped them again, and again. She thought they were beginning to look dry. She put the tea towel neatly back over the towel rail. She ran her hands over the shiny surfaces of the cup and saucer. They still felt wet. She picked up the tea towel and tried again. The tea towel was now wetter than the cup and saucer.

In the vacant, echoing building of her mind a problem was beginning to form.

"Oh, Susannah," exclaimed Nurse Ramsden, scurrying into the ward kitchen. "Oh, Susannah, my dear. What a mess. Oh what a shame. Your beautiful dressing gown. You'd better come with me and have a bath." She took Susannah by the arm. She led her, void and unresistant, to the bathroom.

Susannah, Susannah, Susannah.

The plangent repetition of this word in her head meant nothing to her.

The young woman walked stiffly. She was going to have a bath. She didn't know why she was going to have a bath. She didn't know why she was going to have a bath until Nurse Ramsden stripped off her flowered dressing gown and flung it on to the cork-topped stool beside the overgrown metal bath, turning the taps on full.

Susannah stared at the dressing gown.

As if somebody had slapped her very hard she remembered who she was.

"My dressing gown," she screamed. "My best dressing gown. It's all covered with blood. What's happened to it? Where the hell have I been? What have I done? It was you," she screeched at the little nurse. "You made me do it. I didn't know anything about it. I don't remember what happened. It was your fault. I don't know where I've been."

"You've been having treatment, my dear," said Nurse Ramsden comfortably. "You haven't done anything. It sometimes brings on our period, that's all that's happened. We've just started a period, that's all. Now, look, we'll have a nice bath and feel better."

Susannah remembered.

"Why the fucking hell didn't somebody tell me I was going to come on? Just look at me. I'm covered with it. Just look at my bloody dressing gown. Why, for Christ's sake, couldn't somebody have mentioned in all the hype, that I was going to wake up looking like a bloody corpse."

"That's it, my dear," said Nurse Ramsden happily. "In we get. We'll just put your dressing gown in this bucket. I expect most of it will come out."

Hopeful but wary Nurse Ramsden handed Susannah a sponge liberally filled with soap.

"Would you like me to wash your back?" she enquired.

"You bloody well dare. I'll scream the place down if you come anywhere near me. I've got rights, you know. They didn't tell me this witchcraft was going to cause me to bleed to death. But since it has, at least allow me to wallow in my own bath. Bloodbath. To bath in my own blood. To dispose of my own bloody blood in my own bloody bath," she howled.

"Of course, my dear. But don't stay in too long."

In Nurse Ramsden's woodland a bright little animal appeared from behind a fallen tree. The sun shone through leafy branches and the ferns moved gently in a warm breeze.

There was always cause for optimism.

Susannah was obviously going to need a few more sessions.

But at least it didn't appear to have done her any harm.

15

This was the time that she liked best.

I don't want anything that belongs to anyone. I don't want anybody else's husband, anybody else's children, anybody else's lot. I am alive, I am here.

Judith felt Hector's arms around her and knew that however torn he was by the human problems which confronted him each day, when they were together at night he was whole.

She lay on her stomach beside him and pressed her cheek against his. Could there be any problem which was insoluble? Could there be any trouble which would make going to bed less than a miracle. She thought not.

"Hector," she said.

"Judith," he replied.

"Hector, when we find our new home I think we should have a cat."

"Not a dog?"

"No, a cat."

"Why not a dog?"

"Well, dogs need too much of people. Not their time, or their care. Too much of themselves."

"You don't want to share me?"

"No. I share you with your patients. But I'd find it difficult to share you with a dog."

"What's different about dogs?"

"I would love the dog too. So I would have to allow you to love him, and allow for your loving him as well as me, and allow for my loving him as well as you, and allow for him loving both of us and not knowing which to turn to."

"You think a dog would come between us?"

Judith thought about this.

"It isn't exactly that he would come between us. It's more that he would complicate our existence."

"Complications sometimes make life richer, like a pattern on a plain carpet."

"We are not a plain carpet. We are a beautiful Persian rug."

"So. No dog." Hector was fond of dogs. Though it had not occurred to him that he would like a dog, now that Judith mentioned it, he did think it would be nice. "If we had been younger, do you suppose you would have felt like that about children?" he asked.

Judith was shocked.

"Certainly not," she replied. "Children are another story. Though I don't think I'd have minded not having any if I'd had you."

"Husband and child," Hector murmured into the duvet.

"But I'd still have wanted a cat."

"So. We'll have a cat. What shall we call it?"

"Depends on what it's like. Lawrence was called Lawrence because he had a prophetic air. Enjoyed feeling the bare earth through the soles of his feet, too."

"How could you tell that?"

"By the way he walked. Every step was a work of art, a delight. And he knew things. He knew things which he didn't divulge." Judith thought that if Hector had been a cat she would have sat all day with him on her lap, just cherishing his proximity. "Mind you, he was a bad bugger," she added.

"Not reliable?" suggested Hector.

"Worse," said Judith. "He was lazy and dishonest. He didn't know what cats are for. Ignored mice. Wouldn't have anything to do with them."

"Perhaps he was simply kind-hearted."

"We could have coped with that. But he dissembled. Brought us all to the back door full of his prowess, showing off. Drew our attention to the corpse of a rat with no back legs and purred triumphantly."

"Pulled it off at last. Justly proud." Hector was pleased.

"Don't you believe it. Merely wanted the credit. He'd found it in the field. It had obviously been dead for some time before he caught it."

"Hmm." Hector considered this. "Perhaps he thought he'd killed it. He may just have had a bad memory."

"Please don't make excuses for him, Hector. He had no conscience."

"We must interview our cat thoroughly. Make sure he has a good character. References and all that."

"He was nice, though. We loved him."

"Most things are a mixture," said Hector. He drew Judith closer to him and pushed to the back of his mind a sudden, terrifying vision of Susannah, unconscious after he had administered the anaesthetic.

16

"You didn't tell me you were going to change me into a zombi." Susannah glared at Hector across his desk.

She was sitting in the second chair, not the one against the far wall, not the comfortable one next to his own, but the chair on the other side of the desk.

"You didn't ask me." Hector wrote a word in Susannah's file and gave her a friendly grin.

Susannah had plaited her hair. Around her neat face the impossibly small tight braids stuck out and hung down, weighed with multi-coloured beads, like a straw hat designed for a carnival. Her hands, moving constantly, seemed less anguished than before, Hector noted. She was wearing a polo-necked sweater made out of some artificial knitting fibre which successive washings had caused to change its shape in such a way that it didn't actually touch her body anywhere but fell in a straight line from the neck to the waist at the front and in the same fashion at the back like a pair of sandwich boards. To complete this illusion Susannah had embroidered in huge uneven letters the words 'Come and look around' across its front and across its back, 'but don't handle the goods'.

"That's a stupid thing to say," Susannah pointed out. "I wasn't likely to consent to a form of treatment that I suspected was going to turn me into a zombi."

"Apart from being a zombi, how do you feel?" Hector looked directly at Susannah with a kind of detachment which concealed the fact that he was making myriad mental notes, as well as writing in the file.

"Awful," his patient replied, irritated by his apparent lack of concern. "I'm fed up. This place is riddled with vegetables and lesbian nurses. I want to go home."

"These vegetables are all here to be transformed back into princesses like you," said Hector, "and though I don't see that it is any of your business, which nurses are you describing as homosexual?"

"Nurse Ramsden, for one." Susannah sulked.

"Nurse Ramsden has a husband who is a miner and two sons, both over six feet tall. Do you feel worried about lesbians?"

"Oh don't talk such bloody rubbish. There's no point me coming to see you if that's the line you're going to take. I'm going home." Susannah stood up and stalked to the door.

Her sandwich board sweater, confused by this sudden activity, swung to the left and then sharply to the right.

"Don't forget your handbag," Hector said.

Susannah turned at the door and retraced her steps to the middle chair. The sweater did a smart military about-turn and began to revolve towards the left again. She picked up her handbag.

"Well, you might as well stay and chat for a few more minutes, now that you're back." Hector fished in his pocket and found his pipe.

"Look, Hector," said Susannah, sitting down again. "You don't mind if I call you Hector, do you? I mean, you can't expect me to take you seriously as a doctor when you need to be told what to do next by the patient. It's nothing personal, you know. I'm sure you mean well. But there's nothing you can do for me. There's nothing anybody can do for me. It's been done. I'm finished. They've finished me off."

"So why don't you remain in the hospital for a bit longer and give it a try instead of hurling yourself straight back at them all?"

"Why the hell should I? I don't want to be a cauliflower and I'm not going to be turned into a zombi again, that's for sure."

"The ECT takes a few sessions before it begins to help."

"How can it help? I'm bunged up like an overloaded sewer."

"It might take some of the bad things out of your mind for a time so that we can look at some of the others."

Susannah fiddled with half a dozen of the long, stringy plaits, then put them sideways into her mouth and sucked at them thoughtfully.

"Supposing I don't want to look at things?"

"Then I can't help you. It's like taking out a thorn, a very painful process but one which will make you feel better."

Hector was having trouble with his pipe. He frowned at it, puffing sternly and lighting one match after another.

They sat in silence.

"I don't know why I bite my fingernails." Susannah looked at them, spreading her hands out on the desk in front of her like two small, pale, battle-scarred starfish.

"I can do something about that." Hector beamed into the bowl of his pipe. It was going.

Susannah stared at him.

"Amputation?" she suggested.

"Hypnosis. Cures the nailbiting and retains the hands."

For a few seconds Susannah felt as she had felt in the interval between the prick of the needle and the jerk of her head.

If her fingernails were beautiful she would be beautiful. She would be like other women. She would be good. She would be free. She would start again.

But it was no use. Gavin was dead. Her father had gone. In any case, she hated her father. Her mother didn't like her. And none of those men meant anything to her, least of all the little prat who had put her in the club. As for her stepfather and her stepbrother, there was no way she could describe what she would wish upon them if she had been granted three wishes.

"You are quiet," said Hector. "What are you thinking?"

Susannah told him.

17

Judith sat transfixed.

In front of her lay the local paper. In its columns she had found an advertisement which she had looked at for some time, believing that it would certainly disappear.

She read it again. Then she read it again.

Her heart was beating like a sail in the wind.

Hector. Darling, darling Hector.

She wouldn't go to this house secretly with Pat and Gill. She would tell him about it. They would go together.

After all, she knew what to expect.

'Country cottage with gardens front and rear. Large sitting room, living kitchen, two bedrooms, two attic rooms, three-piece bathroom, full central heating, lean-to extension, garden shed. This residence in desirable area deserves a visit.'

So. Cecil's shed was still there, up at the end of the field. Cecil's lean-to, built to accommodate his many occupations and the boys' boots, was still there.

She read the advertisement again. Looking at it through tears which obscured the print she felt a squall of feelings pulling her in every direction.

She would live with Hector in the same house in which she had been born.

Central heating. There had never been any central heating. She had dried endless pairs of socks and knickers in front of the fire late at night when her brothers and sisters were in bed. It kept her awake, wondering whether they would be properly aired in the morning, thinking of the children going to school with damp garments clinging to them like polite kisses. She wondered what else had been done to the cottage. When she had visited the village two years ago after losing her job at the factory it had looked very smart outside, sand-blasted and gleaming.

At the foot of the advertisement she found the price. The sail of her transporting emotions hovered, emptied, then filled again. Cecil and Sarah had paid a hundred and fifty pounds for the cottage when they were married. She wondered whether Hector could possibly afford the amount its present owners were asking for it, over fifty years later.

Desirable area. She laughed to herself. There had been the wreckage of the old mill, the weavers' cottages all tumbling down though lovingly cared for, the privvies at the side of the road, potholes in the bumpy lane, no amenities. When she was young it could not have been described as a desirable area.

Perhaps Hector wouldn't want to live there. Perhaps he would feel enclosed and trapped by the spectral happenings which must surely have survived in the thick walls, in the heavy beams, in the worn stone flags of the floors, in the paths and shrubs and trees of the garden, in every cranny of that shabby, hectic place. It must surely still be crammed with the precious crumbs that had nourished the lives of them all. Perhaps Hector would hate it.

But even as these thoughts rounded and slackened in her mind she knew that this would not be the case.

Hector would love it. However it had been modernised, whoever had lived in it since the death of Cecil and Sarah, Hector would love it.

She wondered how big the trees were now. She wondered whether any of Cecil's inventions were still functioning, the hole he had made in the attic floor with a pole for the boys to slide down in the morning, or the structure of metal bedposts planted in concrete to support the sweet peas. The pole had made it easier for the boys to get down to breakfast faster than they could by using the shaky ladder they had to climb up at night. The bedposts meant that the sweet peas could stretch up and on towards the sun abundant with blossom and careless of their own luxuriant weight. She wondered whether his electrical wiring systems were still operating.

There was the complicated speaking tube which was useful in fine weather but introduced the possibility of electrocution if it happened to be touched in a shower of rain. There were the multitudinous burglar alarms festooning each room, which went off with an ear-shattering intensity when a mouse or a spider trespassed over them but which would probably have remained dumb if any burglar had attempted to make an entry.

Judith began to cook the evening meal. Hector's clinic would be over in an hour. She would suggest that he should telephone the Estate Agent first thing in the morning.

On and on over the ocean her anticipations raced.

18

Hector was accustomed to detaching himself from his patients and their problems. It was a necessary rule. He could not possibly survive if he became involved in all the traumas which deluded and unhappy people flung at him from every direction like heavy rain day by day. In his years as a psychiatrist he had become expert. He could listen, assimilate, decide, act, and watch with satisfaction when situations improved. When they did not he suffered, but he was not broken.

Judith had been the only exception. Judith had drawn him into her world. Judith had been his miracle. He had found the answer to her problems and in so doing he had solved his own. He had not ever expected to find a patient whose storm would subside and vanish into the buttercups and meadow-grass of a glorious summer day.

But since he had found one, being human, he had changed his expectations and was now on the lookout for another.

He pressed the buzzer in his office which would inform the reception desk that he was ready for his next patient.

He had been thinking more and more about Susannah.

He had no reason to suppose that what she had told him was untrue. Now that he had honed away the edge of her anger, he could see more clearly the events and attitudes which had caused her to become the disturbing force she was.

The question that his discoveries raised was how should he attempt to alleviate her woes.

The answer to this question was that he must put himself into her hands, her new, unbitten hands, as he had put himself into Judith's hands for all those years. She would demand from him what she needed.

But he knew, still partly detached, watching the scene with his outer, clinical eye, that this was going to be a dangerous course.

Too often already, Susannah, avenging the furies roused within her by the treatment she had received when she was a child, had attached herself tenaciously to any man who was foolish enough to allow himself close to her. She had attached herself to these men as a parasite attaches itself to what it feeds on, eroding away until the rock has gone, the ship has sunk, the leaf, skeletal and limp, has expired and died.

Hector did not wish to become one of Susannah's victims. He must keep his eyes open for signs that she wished to revenge her past by adding him to her list of destructions.

"I like my hands," she said, walking into his office and sitting down in the comfortable chair next to his own.

Hector felt the laughter rushing into his lungs and stomach.

Susannah was wearing a pair of jeans which fitted her slightly bowed, brittle legs in the way a folded umbrella wraps around its handle. Stitched untidily across the seat of this garment was a pink cotton hand, the fingers disappearing under the slight curve which was all that constituted her bottom.

"Are you including the third hand in that happy group or do you consider this one an outsider?" he asked demurely.

"I don't know how you did it, but it worked." Susannah took her symbols seriously and chose to ignore Hector's question. "A week and not a chew. Just look. They'll be long enough to put nail polish on soon. Got to congratulate you. Never have managed that on my own. Been trying for years."

"You have done most of it. Hypnosis only works if the subject is willing. But I can't stop you doing other things instead. Smoking more heavily, for instance."

Susannah's hands were roving about in her handbag like two terriers searching for a biscuit. They emerged with a packet of cigarettes and a disposable lighter.

Hector watched them as they trembled and shook putting the cigarette between her lips, flicking the lighter, nervously replacing the packet and the lighter in the scuffed leather bag, moving jerkily between her face and the ashtray which he slid towards her across the desk.

Her hair, today, was free of its imprisoning braids. It stuck out around her face, crenellated and tangled. It stuck out down her back, blonde except around the scalp where its natural dark brown glowed defiantly. Her hair was scrappy, stiff, tortured, ridiculous.

Hector felt the laughter inside himself turning into something else. He realised that he wanted to wrap this manifestation of destiny's callousness in a cloak of feathers.

"You told me that your father used to beat you," he said carefully, examining the paper-knife that Judith had given him for his birthday. The paper-knife consisted of a brass blade engraved with fruit and leaves, amongst which a few small birds strolled decorously, and a copper handle on which an embossed eagle was standing in a tree surveying a pair of chattering monkeys. He ran his fingers over the handle, wondering at the patient craftsmanship which had survived for so many generations.

"Did he do anything to make up for it afterwards, appear to be remorseful or provide treats or say that he was sorry?"

"Did he fuck. The bastard. I hated him then and I hate him now. If she hadn't been so afraid of him she would have been nicer to me. I'd kill him if he came anywhere near me. I didn't mind him beating me. It was what he did to her. She used to sit with her head in her hands, the tears pouring through her fingers. When I tried to comfort her she pushed me away."

Susannah was trying not to cry. The words were coming out in choking clouds like smoke from a fire when the chimney is partly blocked and the wood is wet.

"Once he locked her in the outhouse in the backyard. He took the key away and went to the pub. I tried to break the lock but it wouldn't budge. I could hear her, whimpering. When he came home he was drunk. He didn't remember anything about it. Asked me where she was. Hit me a few times, then passed out in his chair. It was dark. There was no light in the outhouse. She had stopped crying. There was no sound. She didn't answer when I called. I thought she was dead. I would have killed him if I could."

Hector leaned over and secured one of Susannah's roaming, inconsolable hands with one of his own.

She felt his concern, his calm, as a wounded animal trapped on a cliff ledge feels the tenderness of its rescuer. She stopped trembling.

They sat in silence.

"Your father sounds like a very sad man," Hector said at last. "We have to try to forgive people as we come to understand ourselves and them."

Susannah hurled her rescuer into the abyss.

"Forgive him? Forgive?" She glared at Hector, her neck and shoulders rigid, the muscles on her forearms tense as if she were a woodcarving wearing a thin layer of skin. "Forgive my fucking father? You don't understand at all. You don't bloody understand. If it hadn't been for my father none of it would have happened. If he had been a man instead of a walking shit-house the whole thing would have been totally different. Forgive him? I'd rather die. Forgive him? If he came within a yard of me I'd hack off his rocks with the handiest object and pin them to his left nipple."

Susannah lunged towards Hector and her small, white hand grasped the copper eagle and held it high above her head, its curved brass blade catching the sunlight from the window and creating a yellow butterfly which flitted across the ceiling. Her eyes were crimson with fury. She stopped uttering the noises of speech, choking with rage.

There was a moment in which Susannah's attempts to control her breathing tore at the air as a boulder falling from a mountain tears at the silence of a quiet valley.

The knife in Susannah's hand, Hector noticed, was perfectly still.

He smiled a pleased smile.

"Uh-huh," he said. "Now tell me about your stepfather."

19

Walking towards the packaging firm Judith wondered whether her feelings were creating a white light around her like the ring around the moon.

And yet, there was something . . .

Hector had telephoned the Estate Agent's office and they were to collect the key on Saturday morning and visit the cottage, the cottage in which she had been born and grown up amidst the confusion which had eventually led her to Hector.

The something, like a cloud of frozen breath, hung in the air.

She caught a glimpse of Tulip's sandals flapping ahead of her up the wide, shallow stairs.

Occasionally, not very often, but sometimes, she wished that she still belonged to the garment factory where she had worked for so many years. Remembering those years now, safe with Hector, she wondered how she could have been so deluded. She tried to remember life with Murphy in the isolation of the terraced house on Mackworth Street she had thought did not exist. She considered this situation from which she had not expected to escape, a situation which had been crowded with the anxieties of a lifetime's weary devotion to people who had all gone somewhere else.

I know who I am now. I know who I am, what I am, where I live and the reason for my existence.

I am Judith Jones, the wife of Dr Hector Jones. I give my whole personality, my whole being, to making my husband as happy as he is able to be, as happy as I am myself. I live in a flat in the grounds of the hospital in Farringham and I live there for the sole purpose of sharing the timeless rapport of love.

And now, with the curious meanderings of circumstance, like the flat, hidden wanderings of a canal suddenly revealing trees, bluebells, bridges, mills not hitherto noticed I find my past, my uproarious, impossible past has doubled back and met my present, going in the opposite direction.

"Judith," Mrs Eccles greeted her at the top of the stairs, "could you come with me, please. I want you down here today."

"Hell," Tulip commented cheerfully, "you're on stamps, love. Glad it's not me. They stick to everything bar what you're trying to stick them to."

The something was that Hector seemed a bit distrait. He seemed to have something on his mind.

How ridiculous. Of course he has something on his mind. He has all those sick people on his mind. He has on his mind people who are afraid of their emotions, people who are afraid of their bodies, people who are afraid of death, people who are afraid of life.

What a stupid thing to think. Hector has something on his mind.

The little lungful of air hovered, suspended in her mind.

She settled herself comfortably at one of the tables. Piles of addressed envelopes and assorted stamps waited to be united in correct combinations. Unlike Tulip she always found that the stamps, if you applied just the right amount of water from the damp roller and pressed them firmly, were easy to affix. This job did not present distracting problems.

Of course Hector has something on his mind.

Finding himself with a moment to spare, John the warehouse boy put his arm around Judith's thin shoulders and squeezed.

Judith smiled at him. Young people were beautiful.

"We'll have to stop meeting like this," he said, "my bird has a jealous streak."

"Why don't you marry her?" Judith stretched an elastic band around a bundle of stamped envelopes. John's elbow dislodged the remaining envelopes which fell to the splintery wooden floor, scattering in all directions.

"What on earth for?" John had picked up the envelopes before Judith could rise from her seat. "My mates wouldn't half give me some stick if I got wed. They alter, you know, once they've got you hooked, women. Keep 'em wondering, that's the thing. Marriages always end in the shit. My dad walked out when I was five."

"They don't have to. Some marriages are very happy. You've been going out with your friend ever since I came here. Wouldn't you like to feel that you belonged together?" Judith had begun to sort, wet and fix the stamps again.

"Rolling stone, that's me. Keep the old muscles in trim, football on a Saturday, board to me Mum, keep 'em guessing."

He raised his right thumb and winked at Judith.

"John, what about the card? We're going to need it soon. You're not here to pass the time of day." Mrs Eccles, tall though John was, looked down at him from her elegant height, as a folly on a hilltop looks down at a flustered climber.

It is something new and special that he has on his mind. There is nothing different about him. He is behaving in exactly the same way as usual. He isn't staying out late. He isn't drinking. He is as attentive to me as always. He loves me as much as when he smiled that smile as we exchanged promises on our wedding day.

But he has something on his mind. I know that he has something on his mind. But I don't know what it is.

"Of course, there are things you can do to stop marriages from ending in the shit." John was bending down beside Judith's table, his arms full of bundled corrugated cardboard, pretending to tie the already well-tied lace of his training shoe. "Me great-aunt Agnes never wore any knickers. Kept me great-uncle George on his toes, so to speak, for forty years. Said she liked to be handy. Me great-uncle George didn't live to be a right old man, but when he died, by God, he'd had a happy life."

John picked up a stray bundle, gave Judith a companionable nod without turning to look at her and went on his way towards the piles of cruciform prostrate box-shapes destined for the packaging of Lego toys.

Ever anxious to search her conscience in case adverse situations had been brought about by some fault of her own Judith thought about this.

No. On the whole she felt that whatever Hector had on his mind, it would not be affected one way or the other if she took to living without her knickers.

20

After the first two ECT sessions Susannah found that she was no longer afraid.

On the contrary, she began to look forward to that moment when the needle put a temporary end to her consciousness of anger and frustration. Afterwards, of course, it was always unpleasant until, like a child searching for a familiar face in a strange, empty house, she suddenly rediscovered her personality as she entered one of its rooms.

"I like your new hairstyle." Hector took off his glasses and placed them on Susannah's file which lay on his desk. He noticed that the reading part of their bifocal lenses was magnifying the words, 'stealing babies'. Yes, he must remember to explore that one.

Susannah tossed her head as if to remind herself what the new hairstyle was. She tried a new hairstyle almost every day and sometimes, the days being very similar in hospital, this caused some confusion in her mind. Occasionally, as a mental exercise, she would try to remember what she looked like today without either touching her hair or consulting a mirror. Tossing her head, she remembered that she had two plaits, much thicker than usual as they contained all her hair. These plaits began on the crown of her head and hung down in two large, curved arcs like the horns of Highland cattle. To the extreme end of each plait she had attached a pingpong ball liberally coated with emerald green Christmas glitter. As she tossed her head she felt the reproachful touch of these adornments reminding her of their existence.

"Nothing special. Just something I dreamed up," she replied modestly, pleased that Hector had noticed. "The sparkle scratches, though," she added, being too honest to pretend that glamour was painless.

"And how is the treatment going?"

"I don't like being a zombi. But I suppose it could be worse. I've still got my arms and legs." Susannah's hands were ruthlessly exploring the recesses of her scruffy handbag. They searched all the pockets, opened envelopes, turned cigarette packets upside down and shook them, unfurled crumpled, screwed-up tissues, squeezed half-filled paper bags and finally, in a burst of exasperation, hurled the entire contents of this minor museum across the length of Hector's desk.

Hector, sitting beside her, tried to appear concerned.

"You are looking for something," he suggested.

"Of course I'm bloody looking for something." Susannah continued to voyage amongst the wreckage, her hands darting here and there like hamsters sorting out the wheat from the chaff amongst their comestibles.

"I'm bloody looking for a fag. What did you think I was doing, wiping my ass?" Her pingpong balls trembled with indignation.

"Allow me," said Hector courteously.

He opened a battered silver-plated cigarette box which stood behind his paper-knife and offered it to his patient.

"Oh God, thanks." Susannah removed eight or ten of the cigarettes and, pushing the remainder into the side pocket of her now empty handbag, began to scoop her crumby, obscure treasures off the desk back into its sagging void with one hand whilst attempting to light the cigarette which she had thrust between the smears of mauve lipstick which covered her long, thin lips with the other.

"What did you intend to do with them?" Hector looked directly at Susannah, holding the tips of his fingers lightly on the surface of his desk so that he could feel the blood tingling against the polished wood. It was strange, the sensation that something of you was being passed into an inanimate object.

Susannah puffed vigorously.

"Smoke them, of course. What did you think?" She felt slightly uneasy. She needn't have taken quite so many.

"Not the cigarettes. The children you stole from their prams."

The silence which fell between them was disturbed by the sound of hurried footsteps in the corridor outside, by the sound of quiet, persuasive voices and a low, distraught moaning.

"What's up with her?" Susannah asked.

"She'll be all right. She's a little upset at present." Hector continued to examine Susannah's face, replacing his spectacles so that he could see her more clearly.

"You're a sadistic bastard, aren't you? There's a woman out there breaking her heart. You're supposed to be a doctor and what are you doing? Sitting in here asking me damn-fool questions. Why don't you go out and see to her? She needs some help."

"Possibly someone has taken her baby," Hector said thoughtfully.

"So I took a baby. So I took a few babies. So I took them out of their prams and carried them home. The world's full of babies. If you lived where I live you'd see babies everywhere, sitting in filthy prams, wearing dirty clothes. You'd see babies with pinched faces, babies with vacant eyes, smelling of urine, most of them too unhappy even to have a good cry." Susannah's right hand, its newly-grown, neat fingernails polished the same shade of mauve as her lips, stabbed the ashtray with her half-smoked cigarette as a hungry cormorant's beak stabs the water where it has seen a fish.

"I see. You wanted to rescue them."

Tears filled Susannah's eyes. She was trying to force words which her vocal cords would not release through the almost closed passage of her throat, out into the open.

"I know what it's like to have your child taken away. My child was taken away. But I loved my child. And I looked after him. He didn't run about in clothes that were too big for him. He didn't live in squalor. He knew what it was like to be cared for. But they took him away from me. He was the only human being who meant anything to me. And they took him."

For the first time Hector watched Susannah cry.

The two pingpong balls shook at the extremities of the two plaits and her mauve eyeshadow trickled in two lines down her cheeks so that her face began to resemble a ritual mask designed to portray Grief.

Hector felt the tears in his own eyes.

He handed Susannah his handkerchief.

Her foxglove-coloured nails held it, scrubbing wildly at the foxglove-coloured conglomeration of tears and make-up that streamed down her skin and dripped on to her collar.

They sat in silence again.

Hector thought about his desk. His palms were flat on its smooth surface now. His hands were hot. He could feel the cool wood comforting them, the warmth of his blood making a faint mist around his fingers; he felt himself entering this stricken, used, finished tree, the tree entering himself.

Susannah was looking at him.

"You swine," she said in a cold, controlled voice. "You swine. You did that on purpose."

Hector curled up his hands and smiled apologetically. He could now feel the wood, tranquil as the leaves it once bore, against the first joints and the nails of his fingers.

"Well," he smiled his likeable smile and took off his glasses again, "it wasn't so much what I did as what you did yourself. Our feelings become diverted from one channel to another. We can't cope with the consequences of facing up to their journey down the true river bed so we send them off down one that we have created especially for them. You have just been very brave. You have allowed them to go where they belonged."

"Fuck that for a tale," Susannah replied. But she spoke the words as though they, too, were running along a channel especially created to change the course of something which had built up an intolerable pressure.

And she handed Hector's handkerchief back to him.

"Thanks," she said, turning a lingering sob into a tremulous sigh which became a feminine shrug. "I expect my face looks like a polecat's backside."

21

It wasn't that he found her attractive. How ridiculous. Whatever Susannah had about her it was not a quality of attractiveness. At least, it was not attractiveness in the usual sense. It was more the sort of attractiveness that interesting scents have for dogs, who feel that they must investigate old socks, dead rooks and messages left by other dogs.

Yet he could not forget her, except when she was there, in his office. As soon as she had swung her Highland-cattle-horn pingpong balls out of his office he saw her sitting there again, small and tense in the big chair which was beside his chair on his side of the desk.

He had the clearest possible vision of her life in the poor area of Farringham. He saw her dark, damp house and her efforts to brighten it, her pathetic attempts to give the love that she had been deprived of to other neglected creatures. He knew that whatever she had done that was illegal had been sanctified by her motives. He suspected that for the children whom she had 'rescued' their sojourn with Susannah could have been a perplexingly short venture into the ordinary happiness of childhood.

"Straight across," said Judith from the passenger seat.

"May I stop at the stop sign?"

"Oh, I'm sorry. Of course. I just meant . . ."

"I'm tormenting you."

"Oh, Hector, look at the chestnut trees. They're in leaf already. In another month those pale shoots will have infinitesimal chestnuts on their stems. They start to prepare for renewal as soon as they are born. Don't you think that's wonderful? Don't you think it shows great optimism to start thinking about your progeny the moment you appear in the world?"

Hector slowed the car and drew in to the side of the road. The chestnut boughs leaning over the wall enclosed them.

"Judith," he said, choosing out of the confusion which was beginning to accumulate in his own mind the words which he knew were relevant to this particular exigence, "my love, you are prepared, I hope, for shocks and memories, tricks of time and contrivances of the consciousness."

"In what way, Hector? My consciousness is quite calm. I'm very excited, of course. I'm curious to see what the house is like inside now. But I'm not expecting anything shocking."

"I was merely thinking," Hector replied, "that if we should buy this cottage of yours and come to live in it, I absolutely refuse to sleep with the trapdoor in Murphy's nose opening and closing all night as he breathes in and out beside us." He released the handbrake and the car prowled on down the hill.

"Oh, that's all right," said Judith, relieved. "Murphy won't disturb us. Anyway," she added as an afterthought, "Murphy doesn't exist. You remember that."

22

"What the hell do you know about it? You've never been poor. You've never been had up by the police. You've never cried until you couldn't cry any more and then realised that all you were doing was wearing yourself out and that your mother still wasn't going to help you to get rid of the nits in your hair or show you how to wash your knickers so that the other children wouldn't call you names and refuse to sit near you in the classroom, or let you tell anybody that her swollen, purple face was caused by your sodding father and not by a fall downstairs, or that all you had eaten since yesterday was half a boiled egg and that she had not even eaten the other half because she was saving it for you in case there was nothing tomorrow."

"Susannah," said Nurse Ramsden, "would you like to help me to give Tessa her bath? Poor old soul, she does enjoy a bit of company for her bath, and I'm on duty by myself at the moment so I'd be very grateful. She's heavy to get in and out."

"No, I would not."

"Tessa has had a hard life, too, you know."

"Everybody has a hard life. Everybody except people with money."

"That's not true, Susannah. Tessa's life hasn't been like yours. Or like that. She had plenty of money."

"Then she's a fool."

"Foolish or not, my dear, she needs a bath."

"And I'm not your dear."

"I thought you were complaining that nobody loved you."

"You don't love me."

"I like you better when you are agreeable, of course, but I

wouldn't be doing this job if I didn't love people." Nurse Ramsden's woodland scene was becoming dull and grey, as woodlands do when the sun slithers behind a cloud. At such times Nurse Ramsden felt that the burden of human unhappiness was more than she could bear.

She took Tessa's pack of cards out of her limp, clammy hands and helped her to her feet.

"Come along, lovely," she said, "Susannah and I are going to give you a nice bath."

Tessa's brown eyes, faded around the perimeter of their irises so that the colour merged into the yellowish orange of what had once been clear, firm, white eyeball like the markings on a streaky old alley, rested on the angry figure before her. Its blonde hair was sticking out in all directions, plaited in dozens of tiny, neat, stiff plaits, the end of each tied with a brightly coloured ribbon so that they resembled a badly arranged bunch of garden flowers.

"Nice," Tessa observed ruminatively.

Susannah glared at her.

"She's admiring your hair," Nurse Ramsden explained.

Susannah began to weaken.

"Butterflies," said Tessa.

"Oh, all right," said Susannah. "But if she loses the soap, I'm not groping for it."

"Good lass," said Nurse Ramsden, enjoying a little burst of thicket sunshine. "Come along then, ladies. We may not be Brigitte Bardot, but at least we can be clean."

23

It was still a fairly shabby dwelling inside. In spite of being modernised it had an air of friendly destitution.

Hector walked with Judith and the young woman from the kitchen to the sitting room, listening to the young woman's apologies and enthusiasms and Judith's euphoric response to it all.

"We wouldn't be going if Mike hadn't been moved to Cheshire. We love the house and the garden. Would have been marvellous if the job had been nearer. More money, you see. We could have done some of the repairs and alterations we haven't been able to afford. Needs a bit of mending here and there," she added lamely.

A boy of about six was poking a pile of sewing materials in the corner of the room with a stick.

"No, Tom dear. Don't disturb Titus."

Hector wondered uneasily who Titus was and what he was doing under a pile of patterns and fabric on the floor.

"Spiders, you know. All old cottages have them. But Titus is something else. Nearly as big as a frog. I shouldn't be telling you this." The young woman shifted the baby she was carrying from her left arm to her right arm, picked up the dummy which had fallen from its mouth, wiped it on her skirt and forced it back between the baby's lips as one would force a cork which has expanded back into the top of a bottle from which it was withdrawn some time ago. "There are rather a lot of us. We've had to buy an enormous house in Chester. Nothing in between. We hope there won't be any more now. I shall be looking sixty by the time I'm forty-five. Tied up, you know, at last. But nothing's fool-proof. It would be just my luck to come untied. Ginny, take Gary into the garden and help him to find Mummy's potato-masher. Look in the sand-pit."

A vague feeling of déjà-vu stole over Hector. Hadn't he heard all this before?

"We always had spiders. Mice, too, in spite of Lawrence," Judith said comfortingly to the young woman. She wore an expression of wrapt concentration as she compared the present state of her old home with its state as she remembered it.

"These two plugs don't work. We've never been able to discover why. When we came to live here ten years ago we had the whole place re-wired – a grant, you know. The electrician couldn't sort these two out at all. Said the wires didn't seem to come from anywhere or be connected to anything. Said the system looked like something designed for the instrument panel of a spaceship. Said there were wires under the floorboards upstairs which could have launched a satellite."

Judith nodded understandingly.

"That was Father," she explained to the young woman. "Did you, er . . . did you have any trouble with burglar alarms?"

"Burglar alarms?" The young woman looked surprised. "We have no burglar alarms. There's nothing worth stealing."

"No, we hadn't either. But Father liked burglar alarms. He had one just there, by the french window. See, there's the hole in the ceiling."

"A burglar alarm. I always wondered why that hole was there. I thought it was a bit high up for a mouse. No, Tom, don't torment poor pussy. Go out and help Ginny and Gary to find the potato-masher. Hector's the cat's name. Rather a posh name for such a downtrodden animal, but we feel that he has hidden grandeur."

Hector came to with a start. He had been trying to count the children but was mixing them up. Some of them appeared to be twins.

"My husband's name is Hector," said Judith hurriedly, in

case the young woman should say something that might embarrass them all.

"Oh, really? I've never met a person called Hector before. I mean, it's unusual, isn't it? We have difficulty thinking of names for our animals. We've used them all up on the children."

"That's roughly how I came by it, too," said Hector reassuringly. "My mother was a doctor and my father was a barrister. By the time I appeared there weren't any names left which didn't have unhappy associations for them."

"Funny, isn't it," the young woman mused, shifting the baby back from her right arm to her left arm, "how you associate names with your experience of them? Until now I've always thought of Hectors as cats. But, of course, I'll think of you in future." She gave Hector a wide smile. Her teeth had spaces between them. This lent her an engaging appearance, as if she had been one of her own young. "I'll show you upstairs. It's a bit of a mess, but you'll be able to envisage its possibilities. Of course, the rooms will seem much larger when we've moved out."

Hector thought it was funny, too, how you associate places with the people you have experienced in connection with them. He had decided to buy the cottage, whatever it was like, as soon as Judith showed him the advertisement in the local paper. Now he was doubly certain.

24

Ahead of her stretched the long years, like a straight road drawn to illustrate the rules of perspective, with stiff, military poplar trees marching down each side of it to the far horizon, pale and predictable.

Susannah knew that she was never going to be happy. How could you be happy? What was there to be happy about? Wherever you looked, everything was the same.

There were only two things which broke up that long, straight, depressing avenue. One was the split second of release between the needle and oblivion before the ECT.

The other was her interviews with Hector.

She knew why the first was interesting. It was interesting because it always took her by surprise. No matter how much she thought about these feelings afterwards she could not relive them. She could not induce her taut, rigid body to sense that freedom, that exhilaration, at any other time. In the instant that it happened she was high up, a bird gliding on a breeze in the sunshine. But afterwards, if she tried to feel like a bird, high up, gliding, she could not do so. She could not imagine it. She could not remember it. She only knew that the sensation existed.

It was not only physical. She was sure of this. It was not like being drunk or elated with drugs.

It had something to do with the fact that she was surrendering her will, her problems, her desperation, to others. She was giving up the terrible corpse of her life to a kind of life hereafter, giving up to an ultimate authority the terrible memory of Gavin's death, an event which had, in any case, only been the thin dark line along the top of her tragic landscape.

Not being a religious person she had no notions of atonement. Yet she was conscious, each time, half naked in the flowery dressing gown with its faint bloodstains, that her sacrifice of herself was being rewarded.

The second was interesting because of the nature of the interviews. She found that she had begun to make herself as attractive as possible and had tried to be as relaxed as she could for Hector because she wanted to please him. Why she should want to please him she did not know.

Often he made her suffer. Often he made her remember things which she had tried hard and long to forget. Often he had made her hate him.

But afterwards, she was able to think of these times in a positive way, as if he had pushed her a little further uphill into her own reality.

He seemed to like her.

Nothing that she said shocked him. Nothing made him angry, though she knew that sometimes, when she described events to him which had caused her suffering, he was appalled and angered on her behalf.

This knowledge made her both strong and vulnerable. At first she had deliberately tried to upset him. After a time, as the understanding between them deepened, she began to feel a responsibility for him. She began to play down her experiences, knowing that she hurt him, terrified lest she should destroy him as she had destroyed the other men who had taken to her and be left without even her own tumult to support her.

Susannah, in the intervals between ECT treatment and sessions with Hector, had begun to come to terms with herself. She had begun to realise that the endless road with its unbending trees was all that there was. She had begun to realise that this is the road which everyone must travel and that they must travel it without expecting miracles. She realised that the only help they would get along the way was within their own reach, amongst the little red-backed ladybirds, the slithery creatures, the multitude of wild flowers, herbs, grasses and insects. Susannah began to rejoice in the scented, fragmentary, growing things she found in the undergrowth of the wayside with those regimental giants eternally monitoring their course.

25

"Now Tessa, don't trouble the doctor, my dear," said Nurse Ramsden.

"Oh, Tessa and I will have our game of gin rummy later," Hector assured them in response to the old lady's hopeful question. He managed to fit in half an hour with Tessa occasionally, partly because he was determined that one day he was going to beat her. For one of life's losers she was uncannily successful at cards, an incontestable winner.

"Getcha. Getcha again," Tessa promised, a gleam in her yellowed eyes.

Walking away from the ward towards a rendezvous with Alan Judson, his registrar, Hector considered a philosophical problem.

How do you know whether what you want to do is what you have persuaded yourself it is right to do because it is the right thing to do or because it is what you want to do? We live in a world in which rigid self-discipline destroys its own motive forces. But if we overreact to its rigours and do what we want to do for reasons of self-preservation we risk doing the wrong thing.

He knew that he was hoping to see Susannah, at least to catch a glimpse of her, as she returned from the Occupational Therapy Department. If he told himself that it was good for Susannah to see him about the building in between her visits to his office, he also knew that this was not the only reason for timing his movements to coincide with hers.

"How's it going?" he asked Alan Judson who was pouring his third cup of coffee.

Hector remembered the interview not so long ago when the young man had applied for the job as his registrar. Alan had strolled into his office wearing a brightly checked shirt which featured all the colours of the rainbow, his trousers held up by a piece of string. But, in spite of his odd appearance, his academic qualifications were magnificent, and his references were genuinely warm. One even had a footnote saying, 'Do not dismiss out of hand.' Hector might have been tempted to do just this when Alan walked in looking like an itinerant minstrel for it crossed his mind that such behaviour demonstrated an attitude towards life as fraught with problems as that of many of the patients with whom he was proposing to work.

"N. .n. .not bad at all," Alan replied. "We're g. .g. .going to try some psychod. .d. .d. .drama this afternoon. So if you h. .h. .hear an exp. .p. .p. .plosion from the Recreation Centre it's p. .p. .probably going to be a release of p. .p. .p. .pent-up emotion." He swallowed his coffee like a cormorant.

"Susannah Redfearn in the group?" Hector asked casually.

"G. .G. .G. .God's g. .g. .g. .gift to Anarchy?" Alan enquired.

"I suppose she could be described in those terms," Hector conceded.

"She'll b. .b. .be there."

"Make sure the ammunition isn't live."

"She w. .w. .w. .won't need any p. .p. .props. Just a few choice w. .w. .w. .w. .words."

God's gift to Anarchy. A few choice words.

Thus can our dearest interests be dismissed.

26

"Oh, Susannah."

Hector was not a romantic. On the contrary. He knew from experience that for every man or woman whose life flows like a smooth river along its course there are many more whose lives are hindered by boulders.

For two years his own had been uncomplicated and serene. He had allowed its waters to travel between the rocky banks enjoying a sense of freedom which he had derived from being thus restricted.

Now he was beginning to notice the hazards along the way. Now he had to negotiate the rapids which Susannah was creating for him.

"Well, I suddenly thought, 'fuck it. It's such a nuisance, trying to think of a new hairstyle every day. If I find one that is really different it will do for all the time'."

Hector chewed the end of a biro and gazed at Susannah's head.

He tried to make up his mind in a rational way that he was going to like what he was looking at.

But it was difficult.

Susannah's head was like the head of an undiscovered jungle bird that flits among the exotic blooms unnoticed because it is as gaudy as they are.

At the front, where it had been cut in a long fringe which fell over her eyes, it was emerald green. Standing up along the crown, about four inches high, it was the bright pink of fluorescent socks. On the right side, where it had been left to stick out about six inches like tropical feathers, it was turquoise. On the left side, where it was brushed back smoothly and appeared to have been glued to her head, the hair was pure white with black ends and as she turned her head to give him the full benefit of her coiffure he saw with a cold shock that there was no hair at all at the back. Her head had been shaved completely and a large, evil-looking eye had been tattooed on the scalp.

He gave himself a moment to assimilate this vision. Then he wrote a word in Susannah's file.

"Good, isn't it?" said Susannah.

"Uh-huh. It's good," Hector responded numbly.

"I mean, you'd notice me in a crowd, wouldn't you? I don't just look like anyone."

"I'd notice you."

"And you'd think, 'there's somebody different'."

"I'd think you were different."

Susannah hadn't expected all this acquiescence.

She rubbed the smooth surface of her bald space and added ruefully, "The trouble is, nowadays, to be different you have to be so different."

"It worries you, the idea that you are just like everyone else?"

Susannah gave this question a moment's consideration.

"I am different, anyway," she said soberly.

"In what way?"

"Well, for instance." Susannah felt the ordinary burden of maternal grief descending upon her like the ceiling of a room with no doors or windows. "How many people do you know who kill their children?"

She stared at Hector, a defiant stare. The walls, too, were closing in on her.

Hector fiddled with his paper-knife, put it down and offered her a cigarette. The cigarette box was one which had been bought at a flea market by Judith's mother Sarah. Sarah had never smoked but she had treasured this compact, silver-plated brass box with its wooden interior and one of the few household chores that she performed regularly was to polish it, thereby removing more and more of the silver and exposing more and more of the brass. For some reason, possibly because her mother had exhibited this rare streak of domesticity in relation to the box, Judith had kept this object and it had found a home on Hector's desk. When he was allowing his patients to talk he would place his hands on the parts from which the silver had been worn, vaguely trying to establish how it had been handled in order to deteriorate in precisely the way it had.

Susannah took several cigarettes, caught Hector's eye and replaced all but one.

Hector lit the orphaned cigarette and watched Susannah breathe in deeply and exhale the smoke through her nostrils.

It occurred to him that Susannah had an exceedingly beautiful face, fine and delicate, smooth as a porcelain mask, the bones under the clear skin honed to a kind of tilted, poised query; a tender, vulnerable query.

Oh my God. That eye.

"In what way did you kill Gavin?" he asked.

Susannah began to cry. It was not the angry choked crying which he had so far been able to extract from the storm of her psyche but a quiet, dry crying. It was the sort of crying that one might associate with the shocked victim of a bomb outrage who observes that his legs have been blown off but does not know why this observation should make him cry.

Hector knew that unless he could comfort Susannah he was finished.

But he also knew that he must go on.

"I can't live without him. I want him back. Where is he? Who is looking after him in all that space? I want to put my arms around him. I want him to tell me his troubles so that I can love him better. I tried to take everything that hurt away from him. I wanted him to be happy."

Susannah was not herself. Sitting in the chair beside Hector, the cigarette burning closer and closer to her nicotine-stained fingers, she was not trying to be different. She was not trying to coerce the world into a state of fury which would stir her to forget that nobody could help her, that nobody would ever know how guilty she felt, how responsible she felt, how empty she felt.

She was simply expressing the grief of any homely little

mother of conventional appearance from a conventional home in which she led a conventional life and into which the obscenity of her child's death had lurched like a drunken jackboot. Susannah, her rainbow-coloured head bent low so that the faint curve of her thin neck continued like a suppliant arm which ended in the apparition of that profane eye, was expressing a mother's misery.

Hector took the cigarette from her fingers as it was about to scorch her then held the small, gaunt hand.

Lost in his it remained impassive.

They sat in silence.

"Of course, you know," he said quietly, "that Gavin's death was an accident, that you were not in any way to blame."

"I know," Susannah replied. "I know, but I don't believe it."

"The man in the car was charged with dangerous driving."

"But I could have made him more afraid so that he would have been more careful. I thought they were lying to me, you know, that he wasn't dead."

"But now you know that they were not. You know that you will never forget him, but that you will remember his seven years as seven years of happiness. You did everything you could to make them happy for him. You also know that you are very young and can have another child, a whole family of children."

Wide awake and aware again Susannah's hand leapt from its nest and vanished.

"You must be bloody joking," she shouted. "Let myself in for all that bloody sterilising and feeding and scraping shitty nappies. Let myself in for knitting, and screaming in the night, and wiping noses, and worrying about how long the shoes will last, and changing wet beds? Let myself in for going out to meet them from school, and feeling their foreheads, and wondering whether the spots are measles, or chickenpox or rabies or smallpox, or fleabites, or heat lumps? You must be bloody joking.

Anyway. To have kids you need a man. I'm not letting any

sodding male near enough to recognise me, let alone father my children. So if that's all you can say, save it for the next imbecile who comes wandering in to enjoy your magical powers. I may be green, but I'm not a steaming cabbage."

Clutching her handbag Susannah slid out of the big leather chair and stalked across the room, her turquoise side slightly flattened as if the nervous energy which had gone into this interview had taken all the stomach out of it. Her black and white side, less sleek than it had been, lolloped below her ear, her leering bald eye glared viciously at Hector from the back of her skull as she reached the door.

Making a note in the file Hector smiled his wide smile.

A great feeling of elation swept through him as a wave gathers itself together before rising, bottle-green and glacial, to crash towards the shore.

27

"Who wears purple lipstick?"

Judith was sorting out the laundry, putting coloured clothing together, neatly piling white garments on one side and things which had to be washed by hand on the other. The clothing lay around her in derelict heaps, as laundry will. She held up Hector's handkerchief.

Hector felt himself turning pale. It was not a cosmetic feeling. It had nothing to do with the colour of his skin.

He made a swift examination of his conscience, passing the hands of his mind over it as he would pass his hands over the body of a patient, palpating, searching, testing.

Of course, it was ridiculous. His conscience was perfectly in order, regular pulse, steady heartbeat, clear complexion, bright eyes.

Then why did he have this sensation of pallor, this intuition that things were wrong? It was not any kind of sickness, not something definite with explicable symptoms and a possible diagnosis.

It was more a feeling that he was about to be ill, that his conscience, though it appeared to be in the best of health, was harbouring a germ which was going to render it extremely unwell.

"Oh, that's my friend Susannah," he said.

"Is she any better?"

Judith was concerned. Hector did not often talk about his activities in the hospital, but he had mentioned Susannah. He had mentioned her when a large bruise arose where Susannah had kicked his shin during their first interview. Judith had indignantly applied Germolene to the wound. He had mentioned Susannah when she inaugurated a general exodus through the hospital gates on the occasion of her first ECT session. He had also described with some enjoyment the effect of her sartorial experiments.

"Yes and no. She's got no hair on the back of her head at present."

"Oh Hector. Shaved it off with a razor?"

"Trying to excoriate her past."

"Would she like something to put on it?"

"She's put something on it. An eye. To replace the hair. And her past."

"Tattooed? Oh Hector. How awful."

Hector looked at his wife. He tried to remember who had said that a poet was like the wind, invisible until it moved through the trees.

Judith was like the wind. One was conscious of her presence in the day's heat, conscious of the comfort of her, conscious that she was caring and thoughtful and keeping life's temperature at a bearable level. But her personality was visible only in the things she did, the tasks she performed with her hands, the stories that she told, which whether they were fact or fantasy gave an embodiment to the Judith who had no shape or colour of her own.

She put Hector's purple handkerchief in a bowl of water by itself and added some bleach.

"She's been doing very well, letting off steam," Hector explained, indicating the handkerchief.

Sorting shirts, blouses, pants, towels, Judith paused for a moment.

"I can remember how hard that is," she said.

"Well, she's not the way you were." Hector took his pipe out of his pocket and began his ritual match-lighting ceremony. "She's much closer to the surface than you were. The difficulty lies in helping her to express the relevant grievance. She goes all round the houses hating things that have nothing to do with her distress."

"Poor child. Losing her little boy like that. No wonder she is so unhappy."

"It began long before Gavin's death. His was just the hand

that touched her as she stood on the edge and caused her to fall. But enough of Susannah," he said.

Exactly. Enough of Susannah. Enough of Susannah. I've had enough of Susannah. I wish she would get off my back. I wish she had never pirouetted into my clinic. Why didn't they just send her to jail? It's all very well for social workers to suggest that she would benefit from psychiatric help. But before Susannah benefits from any kind of help she eats the helper.

"What did Helen say in her letter?" he asked.

"Oh Hector." The breeze that was Judith soared and lightened and stirred. "Isn't it lovely? She'll be here next month. Next month Helen will be here. Then there'll be the baby. We must be all ready for them. The cottage will have children in it again."

"Mind you," Hector mused, remembering Titus and his tormentors, "it hasn't exactly been bereft of them."

"No, I mean our children," said Judith.

And Hector, loving the breeze and feeling the caress of the word 'our', stirred in the purple handkerchief from which the stains were spreading in widening trails through the bleach with the end of a spoon.

To hell with Susannah.

But he still felt pale. His conscience still warned him that it was not at its best, like a grumbling appendix.

28

Susannah knew that something had happened to her.

It was not simply that she no longer felt the continual flood of anger rushing through her as a torrent of water rushes through a narrow space. It was not that she had been transformed by the primitive excess of the ECT. It was not that she had fallen in love with Hector, though in fact what she felt about him was probably the nearest approach she had yet made to falling in love.

It was something much more complete and inexplicable than any of these things.

Susannah, while apparently rejecting all Hector's attempts to change her way of thinking, had quietly absorbed a great deal of Hector himself.

She lay in the grass, her tattooed eye pressed against one of Judith's patchwork cushions, her discarded clothing in a bundle beside her, her thin white body in its bra and brief knickers drinking the sunshine as a hungry boy drinks his school milk. Hector lay beside her, the grey hairs on his chest gleaming in the bright light.

On the other side of Hector lay Judith, her skirt hitched up, her legs turning a pale ochre colour in the intense heat.

A breeze stirred the seedy grass and the small purple clover flowers, and the hawthorn hedge, and the ash leaves, and seemed to lift the weight of the air from her bare torso like a blanket and then drop it gently over her again.

Hector had told her the names of the hills which surrounded them. Judith had rubbed sun oil on her pale body. Pendle, like a wise elderly man, watched their abandonment to the infinite kindnesses of earth with the sort of approval that the old rarely have cause to lavish upon the rash proceedings of the young.

She could hear the sheep from every part of the landscape singing like a Welsh choral society.

"Listen to the sheep," she said.

"Just been shorn. Glad and sorry," Hector explained.

It had been Hector's idea.

"Judith, my love." He had been hesitant.

Judith knew that he was about to make one of his momentous proposals.

"Judith, since it's the holidays and you're not working and it's a glorious day, how would you feel about taking Susannah out? I've just seen her wandering around the hospital grounds looking like a spectre that can't find anyone to haunt."

"Oh, what a good idea. Over to the other side of Pendle, through the winding lanes. Find somewhere for a picnic."

Hector had thought about Judith's childhood, the family excursions with one car driven erratically by her aunt Iris, who always lost her contingent and had to be waited for every few miles in spite of being told to keep Cecil's car in sight ahead of her. Judith remembered these excursions and could bring the same enjoyment to similar excursions now, an unprecedented excitement for him, as his childhood had been singularly lacking in imaginative treats. He had thought wryly that in some ways he and Susannah were equally deprived.

"She told me the other day that she had never been further than the outskirts of the town."

The faint sounds of the countryside chimed around them like an orchestra of wine glasses filled with water on which a melody is being played. Somewhere a farm dog was barking, a faint comment on the utterly peaceful air, like somebody saying over and over again,

"Nice, nice, nice, nice, nice."

"You're quiet, Susannah," said Hector, squinting at her through his fingers. "How do you like your very own countryside?"

Susannah held on to the grass at her side of the rug.

"Oh, it's all right," she replied.

She experienced a strange rocking sensation, as if the ground underneath them had been moving very slowly, like a branch swinging in the light wind, cradling its burden of leaves.

"Gavin would have liked it," she said.

"Oh, look," said Judith. "A red admiral."

Susannah sat up and watched the butterfly making its way along the hedge.

It could go on forever, endlessly rising and falling, drifting and fluttering amongst the thistle-tufted fields under the hot sky with its big friendly clouds. She could see the sun's rays encompassing them as the curved bamboo barriers of a bird cage enclose a bird, enwrapping the circle of the hills, the trees, the fields and the landscape's slowly moving creatures, human, bovine and canine, to say nothing of the horses and the sheep.

"I feel like that sometimes," she said.

She spoke the words as if the grey, lichen-covered boulders had drawn the words out of her against her will.

"You should feel like a butterfly all the time," Hector protested swiftly, "twenty-six years old and beautiful and intelligent. You should be hovering through time as if all there were to worry about was the next flower."

"You must be bloody joking. Precious few flowers where I come from."

"Flowers are in the mind," Judith murmured slowly, picking a piece of clover and leaning across Hector's stomach to place it on the cushion in front of Susannah's nose. "Flowers are all the good things that we store up and remember. Flowers are moments." She looked at Hector's face and felt a sense of exhilaration which she expressed by touching his chest with the hand which had just given the clover to Susannah, remembering his smile among the flowers on their wedding day.

Hector enclosed her hand with his and opened his eyes for an instant to survey his women.

Susannah was watching them.

She shouldn't have come. She didn't know why the hell they had invited her. They only wanted each other. Flowers. Bloody flowers.

Hector saw the peace draining from Susannah's face.

He took her hand with his free one and clasped it against his chest next to Judith's.

"And when do you feel like a butterfly?" he asked.

Susannah relented.

"More like a bird, really. When the needle goes in before the ECT." She could feel the soft hair of Hector's chest where her hand was being trapped, cautiously, as one would hold a bird.

With a shock she heard herself adding,

"And now."

They lay in the sun, each considering the implications of this remark.

A passing sheep stared at them, as well he might. They were three strange-looking humans: a thin silver-haired middle-aged one with her skirt hitched up (and did she realise that her legs were going to get sore?); a small, young one with hair which looked as if it had been treated to a festive sheepdip, and an eye where no eye should ever be; and a large ram-human between them keeping them all entwined with his big human hands.

"Poor little soul," thought Judith, "she is only beginning to catch the beginnings of being happy."

"I must be mad," thought Susannah, " I must have been mad to say a thing like that."

And Hector, struggling with his emotions, held the two hands as if by holding them he could share the stability which his patient mind had afforded these two, other, struggling consciousnesses.

Nothing mattered.

There was nothing except the soaring and gliding of the planing hills.

29

After that nothing was ever the same again.

Judith devoted herself to Susannah as she had once devoted herself to the throng which was her family.

Susannah was at first invited to meals at the flat, then when she was considered well enough to spend weekends away from the hospital she was invited to spend them with Hector and Judith, and by the time the cottage had been legally transferred from the ownership of the young woman with many children, a spider called Titus and a cat called Hector, and her husband, to Dr and Mrs Jones it had been accepted that one of the spare rooms in the cottage was to belong to Susannah.

"We can't let her go back to her old haunts now," Hector had said.

"Of course not. She must live with us. There'll be plenty of room. That house stretches, anyway. We once had fifteen inhabitants. Not on a permanent basis, of course, only for a few months. Father organised a rota – so many here, so many there, meals in three different rooms, one of them in the attic. The boys all had to sleep on the floor. They used to make a terrible fuss when Nicky took his socks off. 'Nicky, put your feet in your sleeping bag,' they would shout in a chorus. Poor Nicky. He couldn't help his feet. But they permeated. You know what boys' feet are like."

"I know." For the first time in his life Hector was not having trouble with the feet which he had suffered from since he was a boy. Judith dealt with his socks as sternly as she had dealt with all the other socks she had been exposed to during her years with men and boys.

"She needs to be looked after, and we'll look after her,"

Judith went on. "Living in the country will transform her."

"No. We don't want any more transformations. We just want her to decide which of her many transformations up to date she wishes to adopt as an enduring expression of her personality. That way we shall know what to expect when we hear her coming down to breakfast in the morning."

"The eye is disappearing nicely."

"When the pink and green has been gone long enough for us to discover what colour her real hair is I shall feel happy. More important than these dazzling attempts she has made to be somebody else is the cool, grey, serious effort she has made to accept herself and her misfortunes. Her real hair will be a lasting symbol of that acceptance. She is getting better. She is definitely getting better. Until she feels able to strike out for a possible life of her own, if you can cope with the difficult times, we'll help her as much as we can. But we mustn't expect miracles." Hector took off his glasses and polished them on the sleeve of his shirt.

"I think you've already achieved miracles."

"She's done it herself. There is something miraculous about her. She's like the grass and wild flowers in New York bursting through the concrete."

"She's always very nice to me."

Hector stopped taking books from the shelves he had put up in the flat and watched his wife. She was packing a suitcase.

He watched her awkward hands. Her hands seemed to acquire a life of their own when they were carrying out a task. They took on a new expression, like the face of someone changed from its dull familiar appearance to sublimity by an act of love.

What Judith's hands performed were acts of love. Her hands, if you looked at them in repose, were plain and unexciting. Lifting, stirring, cutting, sewing, fulfilling any particular function they became animated, as if being useful made them happy.

Now they were folding garments and placing them carefully one upon another as if it mattered deeply that they should be taken to their new home fitted together comfortably. She picked up a checked shirt of which he had always been very fond. Before laying it on the bed to arrange the sleeves down the back she examined a frayed part of its collar critically and he knew that as soon as they were settled in the cottage the shirt would appear on her knee in the lamplight and by patching the frayed piece she would show ever afterwards her understanding of his fondness for it. Any other woman would have urged him to discard it. Judith would go on repairing it until the repairs had recreated the entire shirt.

She would do the same thing with Susannah. Already she had made her a new skirt to replace the one with the torn pocket, judging correctly that Susannah did not cling to this because she was fond of it, but because it was there. And what her hands did for Susannah's wardrobe her mind would do for Susannah's mind.

The two had something very profound in common.

Hector had thought long and hard about what the two women shared. He knew that they both needed to care for people, to provide an atmosphere of comfort and security for creatures who lacked it. He knew that they were both resourceful and imaginative. He knew that they were both tormented by fears and insecurities of their own. He knew that their opposite way of expressing these anxieties – Judith's by punishing herself and lapsing into unreality, Susannah's by punishing others and entering violently into the kind of reality that most people avoid – was only a chance, a fortuitous difference in their constitution. He knew that Judith, given the security of his presence, would strengthen Susannah's newly developing understanding, and that Susannah, with Judith's support, would have much to give in her own way.

Like many very intelligent people, Hector, in his meanderings through the psyches of his wife and his patient, while exploring interesting little country lanes and urban alleyways, had missed the main road, or two main roads.

He had failed to notice that the first bond which joined

Susannah and Judith was their love for him. And he had also failed to wonder, as she improved and progressed, what Susannah would give back, and to whom.

"Yes," he said thoughtfully, feeling as if Judith's hands were caressing him as they patted the checked shirt into its corner of the suitcase, "she can be very beguiling when she likes somebody. Terrifying, when you think of it."

30

It was while they were in the process of moving from the flat in the grounds of Farringham Hospital to Judith's old home that Hector saw the birth of ordinary, healthy despair in Susannah and realised, to his dismay, that there was nothing more he could do for her.

He had known that the ghost of Murphy might haunt Judith in the cottage. It had not occurred to him that every spectre she had ever encountered might descend upon Susannah there.

Hector did not feel encumbered by the formalities of his profession. He knew that he had to work within the framework of established medicine. He knew that for his own sanity he had to regard the people he came across as patients. He knew, he had always known, that he could only do so much for each human being who drifted like a rowing boat without oars into the waters of his awareness. With Judith it had seemed simple and natural to supply her with oars but to keep her constantly within his confines. He was in love with Judith. He had foreseen the dangers but met them as they arose, and dealt with them, and enjoyed the excitement which her ability to steer her own course through the lifting mists of unreality gave him, and the stability which her untethered dependence and joyfulness created.

But Susannah was different. Susannah knew, as he did, that he could go so far and no further. She knew, she had always known, that her moments of voyaging in happiness were and would be short-lived. Had he, though, understood what watching her suffer constantly would mean to him? Feeling her depression he felt the burden of the circumstances which had caused it. Feeling her despair he despaired for the helpless mother who had given Susannah life, and then withheld the care which would have made it worthwhile. He despaired for the child whose death had extinguished the breeze which could have kept her embers glowing, for the father who had been a failure to her and a failure to himself, for the stepfather to whom she had seemed just another insoluble problem. He saw Susannah every day in the company of his beloved Judith, trying to be practical, trying to be helpful, trying to be positive, trying to supply Judith with the daughter she had not given birth to. He saw her trying to be cheerful, trying to add to a sum of contentment which she could appreciate only too well, but from the outside. He saw her pale, composed face becoming more beautiful as her hair grew brown and shining and her unbitten nails rested, poised, on the quiet little hands. The terrible eye had gone from memory. And as he saw these things he suffered as he had not suffered before.

For Susannah there would be no happy ending. For Susannah it was a question of accepting the unacceptable, of coming to terms with the impossibilities of what her life had offered her.

It wasn't that Hector wanted to solve the problems of the universe. He had grown out of that while he was an optimistic but unfortunate adolescent. But he was profoundly disturbed by his own inability to cure the sickness which had darkened the skies over this one young woman who was being lapped to and fro across his harbour. It seemed too cruel to him. It seemed inconceivable to him that there was no way in which he could help her to find a motive for living.

He watched her listlessly planting geraniums in Judith's old chimney pots and pulling the weeds out of the flower beds, and busying herself in a lethargic way, following Judith's example but without Judith's enjoyment. He watched her, tiny in a pinafore which wrapped around her twice, gamely painting the kitchen walls. He watched her, taught by Judith, attempting to prepare food which looked good enough to eat. He watched her sitting with her tongue protruding slightly, her small fists taut with effort, learning to knit. He heard her swearing diminish as she became involved in the kind of tasks which animated Judith. And as he watched her he knew that she was doing all this as a drug addict has another fix, a drinker another drink, a smoker another cigarette, a gambler another throw; it was all to keep at bay the encroaching darkness, the thick empty black space which falls upon minds exhausted with the depression of overactivity, social indignation and their own impotence.

Oh, if Hector had been God he would have started the whole performance again, making sure that all the Susannahs were born with flying feelings and kept them for ever, as they progressed from the arms of enchanted young mothers and fathers and brothers and sisters to the arms of adoring husbands and children in such a way that their best energies were released and rewarded.

But Hector was not God. And the only solution that came to him was an idea he began to cherish that one night when Judith was asleep he would climb quietly up the attic staircase to the boys' old bedroom which Susannah was making uniquely her own and spend the night cradling her in his arms as he would have liked to cradle the whole of humankind.

What this would achieve he couldn't imagine, except to relieve his own wish to comfort a misfortune in which he felt himself to be totally involved.

31

Susannah sat in her attic bedroom. The sun fell through the skylight and a faint sandstorm of dust hovered in its weight, the motes glittering as they progressed haphazardly between the floor and the glass. The young woman had left pieces of carpet which Judith had gladly accepted to cover the floors until they had time to buy new ones, and Susannah and Judith had thrown them over the clothes line and whacked at them with sticks. But a whole generation of dust still flourished. Susannah did not mind the dust. It took what strangeness there was away from her new retreat with its tidy bed, the posters which she had attached to the walls with sellotape and the white furniture. Judith insisted that as it was to be her home for as long as she wished to remain there it must be furnished according to her taste, and Susannah had chosen what she would have liked to possess when she was a young girl.

She felt as if this furniture, the white dressing table and the wardrobe with raised gilt patterns was a symbol of something that had happened to her. It was white, white and gold. She examined her new fingernails, neatly manicured and without polish. Judith had tactfully suggested that such lovely hands did not need adornment and she had accepted this advice with a kind of relief.

She looked at her new hair in the mirror. It was growing longer and browner and shinier every day. She wondered why she had spent so much of her life bleaching and dyeing it, torturing it into ridiculous shapes. Something of the old Susannah stirred in her mind. She began searching for epithets to describe the Susannah it was examining. But it settled again, as the dust was settling, a sparkling collection of finished fragments peacefully descending, all the anger gone out of it.

Her small face peered intently back at her from the mirror in the carved oak frame which Hector had fastened above the dressing table, on the stone chimney-breast. She stared into its pale eyes, eyes which reminded her of her son, and became lost in a world of remorse and sadness. The night before, in order to escape from the general chaos for a time, they had walked down to the reservoir in the twilight and sat under the trees on a wooden bench. Lights from the road at the top of the hill shivered across the water like trembling pillars unsure whether they could carry the burden of its blackness. Bats swept towards them and wavered away again unsteadily as their radar apparatus warned them of the human presence. When the first one crashed out of the leaves Susannah, who had never seen the numinous shape of a bat before, covered her face with her arms in the semi-darkness. Hector had gently removed this blindfold and the three of them watched the spastic antics, each of them with their own thoughts.

"Like the flying feeling," Susannah had thought. "Not smooth gliding; drifting into nothing. More the way we go every day, not knowing what will hit us next."

"Beautiful," Judith had thought, holding Hector's warm hand, "a beautiful tranquil night with all its creatures living their untroubled lives in the darkness."

"Black," Hector had thought, "it's all black. Even the frogs by the water which must surely be a brilliant green and yellow are black in this light, this lack of light. That's what depression does. The colour goes."

Susannah was afraid. She was about to experience something else that was new to her, like the bats. The repeated patterns of her twenty-six years were over. Judith and Hector did not either demand or give to her in a way that was possessive. So she had stopped pretending. Judith had taken the void that was Susannah's mother and filled it with practical satisfactions. With Judith Susannah did what she had longed to do with, and for, that thin, beaten woman when she was a child. But it was too late. Doing these little chores only increased her loneliness. She liked Judith. She liked Judith very much. Judith did all these things for Hector. Who could she do them for? Her own mother? Impossible. She did not ever want to go back to her mother's critical ineffectuality, to her odious half-brother and her dismissive stepfather. Perhaps they would treat her differently. No. They would be the same, even though she had changed. So she worked with Judith in the house knowing that Judith was doing things for Hector and that she, Susannah, was not even doing these same things for herself. She was just doing them, as the women in the ward had knitted, mindlessly, in order to hurry along the sluggish passage of time.

And yet. And yet. Here she was with the gold and white symbols of a possible elegance of living which she had never even contemplated. And the remorse and sadness which filled her were an extension of those visions of her mother, hopeless, defeated, and Gavin, a calculating child to everyone else but in her eyes the epitome of love. The extension of these feelings transformed them into a frightening mixture of hope and perplexity. She knew that the old Susannah, loving Hector, would have taken him easily from Judith, used him, and then destroyed him, as a cat destroys a shrew, although it has no use for the creature. She also knew that this course of action was out of the question. She also knew that nobody else but Hector would fulfil her need to live. She knew that there was not, and never would be, anyone else with whom she felt safe as she felt safe with Hector.

She watched the dust in the sunlight turning very slowly like a giant breath of air in frost and knew that, not for the first time in her life, she now had within her reach a relationship with a man which she could not take up, which was forbidden. There had been her father, there had been her stepfather, there had been Gavin. And now, she wanted Hector. She did not want him for what he could give to her. He had already given her what he could. She wanted him in an unfamiliar way which was much worse. She wanted him to give things to. She wanted to live for him. She wanted to be alive for him. She was alive for him.

This realisation appalled her.

The remorse, the sadness, the hopeless hope revolved in her mind like the dust in the sunlight.

32

Judith was not, as Hector had thought she might be, haunted by the presence of her imaginary husband, Murphy, in the cottage in which she had been born and spent the first half of her life. She was, however, haunted.

As she lay beside Hector she listened to the sound of his breathing, conscious as she had always been within those thick stone walls, of the infinitesimal space which divided life from death. Life was so fragile. Death was unconquerable, always close.

Wide awake she searched for signs of light in the dense sky beyond the hill at the top of the garden. She could distinguish the black shapes of the two trees which her father Cecil had planted sixty years ago. They touched the horizon where a first, paler blue of the dawn was holding the sleeping grey of the attenuated clouds.

Soon the colour would begin to seep along the ridge of the field. Soon the early risers would start the reassuring business of the day. Soon there would be a small, subdued bustle, the sound of the first car in the village street, the rattle of a milk bottle, a little cough from Susannah in her attic room above them, the squabbling of two watchful cats.

Hector's breathing was so quiet that she pressed her face against his back to feel the warmth, the halcyon presence of his continued reality, the reason for her equilibrium.

She knew that she would have been an impossible mother. Even with her brothers and sisters in this house she had been constantly and infuriatingly on the alert. 'Judith the Vigilant', Cecil had called her, monitoring as she had the progress of the nights, waking and standing silently in the doorways of the bedrooms listening to the children's breathing, keeping at bay the perils of the unknown by the power of her need for all to be well.

If she had been able to do so without disturbing them she would have wakened each of the house's sleeping occupants at regular intervals to ensure that they were all right, that they were happy and content in their absence from the consciousness of day. She knew now, as she had known then, that this need to be comfortable in her mind about everyone's comfort was senseless, merely a projection of her own anxious, fearful self. She knew now, feeling the continuation of her own well-being in the regular movement of Hector's breathing, that the quivering of the last few stars in the sealike blue of the dawn was all the reassurance she would ever get that all manner of things would be well.

He turned over as if in response to her wakefulness, enclosed her with his arm and murmured,

"Hello. Go back to sleep. Even the sheep are dozing."

Judith felt as if her formless prayer was answered, as it was always answered by Hector's intuitive understanding.

She closed her eyes and drifted into the rhythm of his sleep, content to let the breathing take care of itself.

Helen was on her way. The house was ready. Soon there would be plenty to worry about during the night.

33

Susannah watched Helen walking towards the front door with Judith and knew that she was going to hate her.

Helen, the same age as Susannah, could have been from a different planet. Where Susannah was pinched, pallid and delicate as a Victorian doll, Helen was robust, sunburned, red-cheeked and tousled. Where Susannah was resentful and over-sensitive Helen was forthright, confident and good-natured. Susannah knew that the world was against her. Helen knew that the world was on her side.

The brass lion above the letterbox gleamed, his polished surfaces catching the afternoon sunlight as though they had been golden fur in the jungle heat. Susannah had spent an hour in the morning rubbing his great countenance with Brasso, rubbing him again and again until under her astonished eyes he had been transformed from a blackish-green dull shadow of himself to his former glory.

Helen stepped into the cottage and exclaimed,

"Oh, Judith, what a lovely home. It brings back all the stories to me. No wonder Father never forgets it. No wonder you all had such a happy time."

"Well, it's yours for as long as you want to stay," Judith replied, "and it is all ready and waiting for a new Holmes, the same as ever." Her heart was beating as it used to beat when the children came home from college, beating with the excitement of loving and caring.

Hector had been manoeuvring the car into the small space around the corner allotted to him by the rest of the village, space for parking being a constant topic among them. He picked up two suitcases and followed Judith and Helen into his house, winking at Susannah who was struggling with a third suitcase behind him.

"Well, it shouldn't be long now. I haven't any idea what to do with it when it arrives, you know. I'm no mother. It'll have to learn to fend for itself."

"You never considered, er . . . not having it?" Hector asked.

"No way. Put it down to curiosity. I'd never want to marry. But a woman isn't a woman until she's had a child, I mean – well, you know what I mean." Remembering that her aunt had never had any children and not knowing anything about Susannah, Helen thought she had better not express her views any further until she had taken stock of her surroundings.

Susannah struggled over the threshold with her suitcase. She was thinking gloomily that it was time for her to move on.

It had been a wonderful month. But she was not wanted here. This was a family affair.

She looked angrily at Helen's huge, taut abdomen pressing against the cotton dress she wore as if it were a forceful wind behind the sail of a small ship urging it on across the white of a smooth ocean.

So there was going to be another baby. Weren't there enough bloody babies in the world? Why did people persist in populating the world with sodding babies? Especially if they didn't know what to do with them. She wondered whether Helen had foreseen the prison cell that she was about to enter.

The house would be reeking with damp nappies, talcum powder and things being boiled. The nights and days would be punctuated with wailing, the terrible wailing which meant that you must leave whatever there was between you and despair and face despair, as you faced the dark snow on the journey home from work on a desolate evening.

"Susannah and Judith have worked very hard to get the little room in order for you, Helen," Hector said, stacking his two suitcases against the wall in the sitting room and taking Susannah's from her to lean it against them. "They've been doing wifely things to it ever since we moved in. Insatiably nest-conscious, the pair of them. I think you'll like it.

Susannah's made you a mobile. Birds. Very pretty. Should entertain the new arrival. Love to make nests, Susannah and Judith. Insatiably nest-conscious, the pair of them," he repeated.

"I'm not. I couldn't care a fuck. It's not my nest," Susannah pointed out.

"No. Of course not. Nothing to do with you. You're just passing through," Hector agreed comfortably. He wondered how long Susannah's predictably rapturous welcome to Helen would last.

"Now then," said Judith, as happy as she had been in her life, "let's have some tea in the garden. You'll need to get as much sunshine as you can, coming from all that heat. Then you must go and have a good rest. There's no need to unpack straight away. Just take what you need to begin with."

Susannah filled the kettle. She'd just make herself useful. She wouldn't actually speak to Helen. Obviously everyone was going to address all their thoughts to her from now on. Why should she bother to be agreeable?

She glared at Helen's robustious face, surrounded by a luxuriance of black, shining hair.

"Now, Aunt Judith, you mustn't fuss over me. I'm a very independent being, you know. I can take care of myself. You just carry on with your normal life. I'll fit in nicely. I don't want you to put yourself out for me. It's all a great adventure, in a way. I hope you'll enjoy the baby. But we're not going to be put out by it. It has to learn to fit in with everybody else. It's not the centre of the universe."

"Like hell it isn't," thought Susannah morosely, pouring the boiling water into the teapot. "Like hell the little bugger isn't the centre of the universe." She filled the four mugs and thrust them ungraciously towards Hector and Judith and Helen. Then she picked up her own and stumped out into the garden.

"She's missing her pingpong balls,' thought Hector, reflecting that at such times her departures had always been more dramatic when accompanied by the swirling garments and the vindictive pigtails.

They followed her outside.

The mesembryanthemums which Judith had planted were reaching out towards the sun, their petals electric with red, pink and gold.

"Look at your geraniums, Susannah," Judith exclaimed. "They never used to grow like that in those chimney pots. You really are good with plants."

Susannah scowled at the geraniums. It was true. She was good with plants. The geraniums in the chimney pots were beautiful.

When she was a small girl there had been nothing that grew in the bleak terraced house. She had longed to bring something living into its dark interior. She had stolen some money from her father's trouser pocket and bought a geranium from the greengrocer's shop and cared for it as she was later to care for her son. When her mother was sitting vacantly in the back room Susannah would talk to the geranium, tenderly removing the blooms as they faded, snapping off the yellowing leaves, keeping the soil soft and watered and, as it increased in size, taking cuttings and spreading them along the brown wooden windowsill in the disused front room until they had taken it over and it had become theirs.

A neighbour, seeing Susannah's garden of hope from the street outside, had brought her a scented geranium and this, too, had flourished, as if it knew that it was being given a whole lifetime's experience of love which nobody else wanted.

But the geraniums which she had grown for her mother had been like the single light of an aeroplane making its way through a very dark sky at night, illuminating nothing, proving simply that light exists. Her mother had never appreciated them or acknowledged that they gave her comfort, if indeed they did.

The geraniums which she had planted in Judith's chimney pots seemed to Susannah to have the peculiarly overgroomed appearance of spoiled children. They had grown extra red, extra large, the leaves extra glossy. It was as if they knew that for them it would never be a challenge to survive, only to succeed and excel in this atmosphere of admiration and acclaim.

Susannah resented the six chimney pots filled with geraniums which she had planted and reared.

"Oh, they are. They're gorgeous," echoed Helen.

My God. What have I got myself into? They told me Aunt Judith was strange. Aunt Judith told me that Susannah was a dear person with a great many problems who needs all our understanding. But they're all crazy. Him as well. Look at him sitting there looking at us all as if he were unravelling a large ball of string. You can stop looking at me like that, cobber. I'm not nuts. I've got all my chairs at home. As soon as this bulge has dispersed I'm off back to the land of the living. Claustrophobic isn't the word for a postage stamp garden filled with screwballs admiring geraniums in rows of derelict chimney pots.

"Gorgeous," she repeated, as if to counteract the flow of her stream of consciousness.

"Those bloody geraniums are ruined. Too much attention. They'd never have managed where I come from." Susannah swallowed her tea as if it were a concoction of poisonous juices, or at best as if it were going to make her puke. She swung off into the cottage to wash the mug.

The oak tree stirred over Judith's flowers in the sunshine. The heat rested on them like a flimsy shawl.

"A bit temperamental, our Susannah," Hector explained apologetically. "But I think you'll find there's more to her than meets the eye when you come to know her." He silently thanked whatever forces moved our destiny that the eye had gone from the back of Susannah's head before the arrival of this self-possessed young Australian. And with all the fervour that he could muster in the easygoing armchair of his psyche he hoped that the new Holmes would be a boy.

34

Three weeks later Susannah was still planning to leave, Hector was still suffering from his masculine isolation and Judith was still euphoric about creation. Helen was merely very large.

The date when the baby was due to appear had passed. The mother was unperturbed by the non-event.

"They tell me that first babies are always late," she said languidly. "In any case, his father was a procrastinatory clod. He's probably all curled up in there reluctant to make a move. Never did anything for himself if he could get somebody else to do it for him. Like father like son. Or whatever. He'll break out when his rations become inadequate."

"What did they say at the clinic?" Judith was feeling the first faint stirrings of anxiety.

"Wait another week then they'll review the situation."

"Have you had any twinges yet?" Hector was trying to light his pipe.

They had just finished their evening meal. Susannah was stacking the plates on the edge of the big stainless steel sink, filling it with water, glowering into the bubbles.

As soon as this bloody baby was born she'd find herself somewhere to go. There was no point hanging around. Nobody wanted her. When the little bastard came she'd be more in the way than ever.

She lifted the plates into the soapy water and began to wash them savagely.

"Dozens and dozens of twinges. Some of them gigantic. But they tell me you know when it really begins."

"Well, they form a rhythm and get closer and closer together, of course." Hector lit another match and sucked at his pipe as if he were extracting venom from a dear friend who had been bitten by a snake. The pipe made bathwater noises and failed to ignite.

Judith emptied a little erection of used matches which had been building up in the ashtray and replaced the ashtray. Hector began to rebuild it at once with the two matches he had used while Judith was performing this task. Judith picked up a tea towel and started to wipe the dishes as Susannah slammed them into the draining rack.

"Perhaps a good walk would help. Let's go down the lane and watch the bats," she suggested.

"That would be nice," Hector agreed, persevering against all odds. "It's been a good sunset. It will be light for another hour." His tobacco remained incombustible.

"I'm not carrying the baby home if it's born on the edge of the reservoir," Susannah muttered darkly.

"I don't think we need to worry about that. They give quite a lot of warning, especially first ones." Judith remembered the long hours beside her mother's bed during the confinements in which her last three brothers and sisters were born.

"What a bully idea. I adore bats. Though I'll bet you've got nothing to compare with our bats downunder." Helen thought that only a collection of loonies would want to stroll off into the gathering dusk to watch the antics of a bat colony by a pond.

However, before they reached the bottom of the hill she began to have other preoccupations. Something was going on inside. It certainly wasn't contractions – not regular, recognisable contractions as she had been led to expect them. It was more a general sensation of movement. By the time they reached the reservoir she was glad to sit down on one of the benches thoughtfully provided for picnickers.

They watched the colours leave the water, then the sky. They watched the bats swerving in and out of the trees.

As they began to make their way back up the hill it was becoming dusky, the light obscuring shapes with a strange mixture of diffused tones of darkness.

Halfway up the hill Helen gave a little cry.

"My God," she exclaimed, clutching her abdomen, "that was a twinge-and-a-half."

"Nearly there," said Hector reassuringly. He had noticed that Helen had lapsed into a mood of thoughtful concentration which was alien to her nature.

"Maybe it's done the trick." Judith began to feel excited. The prospect of having a baby about had filled her with anticipatory joy for a long time but she had not realised until now, when its appearance was imminent, just how much she had been looking forward to it. Who would it look like? Would it be like their side of the family? Helen had said very little about the child's father. She hoped that was not a bad sign. He might be a criminal.

"Oh shit. Another one," said Helen, standing still with her legs braced like a tent peg which is trying to hold down the side of a tent being whipped by a gale.

They all stood still until she felt able to continue.

"Look," said Hector, suddenly observing the possible onset of a crisis, "just make your way steadily on. Don't hurry. There's no hurry. But I'll go and get the car and come down to meet you."

As if to disprove his own words he hurried away into the darkness like an otter who has tested the wind and found traces of hound.

Susannah smiled broadly, knowing that nobody could see her. Serve them bloody well right. She'd warned them.

Hector met them at the top of the hill, his headlights speeding towards them along the lane in an uneven course as it bumped in and out of potholes.

"Here we are then," he announced, as if they might not have noticed his arrival. "Now when we get to the cottage you leap out and ring the hospital to tell them that we are on our way, Judith my love. Susannah, you run up stairs and collect Helen's suitcase. Then we'll go straight away."

They had to wait another minute or two until Helen could raise her leg to climb into the car. The contractions were now coming every three minutes.

Hector was sweating.

When they reached the cottage Helen declared that she could go no further until she had been to the loo.

They extricated her from the car and helped her, stiff-legged like a robot, to shuffle up the stairs. The waters broke halfway.

Susannah was staring.

"Susannah, be a love. Get Helen's bag." Hector was trying to maintain an air of professional calm, as if he often encountered birth in this manner. "Judith, dear, the hospital."

It was while Susannah was running downstairs with Helen's suitcase and Hector was standing outside the front door looking at his watch and Judith was in the kitchen telephoning the hospital that Susannah heard Helen scream, from the bathroom. She dropped the suitcase and ran back up the stairs. As she entered the bathroom Helen hurled herself off the lavatory seat in a shower of amniotic fluid and blood, and by leaping across the room in one bound Susannah caught the baby as it was born, stretching out as a particularly vigilant cricketer at silly point might stretch out to catch a swift, sure ball travelling low towards the boundary.

Within seconds the bathroom in the old cottage resembled, nay, surpassed all its former glory. It had sheltered drunken boys guarded by suspicious dogs. It had seen many a morning after many a night before. It had witnessed the cleansing of many misfortunes. But it had never done duty for a maternity ward.

Hector, having cut the umbilical cord, was disposing of the placenta in a polythene bag and humming a little tune.

Susannah, cradling the slippery baby in a towel, having cleaned away most of the blood and slime, was sobbing uncontrollably, a look of pure happiness on her little face.

Judith, holding Helen's hand as she sat on the bathroom chair, was too overcome to react properly to any one detail, except to notice that Helen's hair had become even more ruffled than it usually was. Reaching up to the bathroom cabinet she removed a hairbrush with which she began gently putting it to rights, murmuring,

"Well, I never. What about that, then? What about that. What a lovely way to have a baby. No fuss, no excitement."

"There'd have been some excitement if Susannah had been two seconds later," said Helen, touching Susannah's hand. "He was about to dive into the loo. Just like his damn father. What an indignity. Entering the world through a lavatory seat."

Susannah was laughing now, laughing and crying and holding the baby as if she had in her arms all the joyous things that she had never quite been able to grasp.

As the ambulance took Helen away sitting up with her newborn infant and Hector beside her carrying the plastic bag with the afterbirth, Susannah and Judith set about putting the bathroom to rights.

It was as if this extraordinary event had crowned the whole landscape of their lives, as the sunset crowns the moors and the trees and the clouds, setting everything aflame.

And when Hector returned, having been given a lift home by a colleague, to inform them that Helen was being kept in hospital for a couple of days and that they could visit her in the morning, he too was jubilant.

He would remember the expression on Susannah's face, always.

At least now the odds were a bit more even.

Susannah had a cause. And he was no longer alone in this female-oriented establishment.

35

"Perfect. Just what you wanted. Exactly right. Judith, flower, you couldn't have found anything better if we had looked forever." Pat and Gill were paying their first visit to Judith's new old home. Pat looked around the kitchen, neat with its solid fuel cooker, flower prints and polished oddments of furniture. Over the stove an old-fashioned airer was suspended, festooned with folded nappies and tiny garments which exuded a faint, soft smell of cleanliness.

"Mind you," she thought, "it's not everybody's cup of tea. No pelmets, no skirting boards. Bare stone walls." She wondered vaguely how you kept bare stone walls clean.

"Like camping," Gill echoed, drifting along on Pat's tide of perception. "Primitive but comfortable." It was comfortable, if you liked that sort of thing. "I'll bet this house has seen a few orgies. How old did you say it was? Two hundred years? It'll have seen a few orgies, this house will, in its day. And a birth on the bathroom floor. I thought my Teddy was going to do that on me. Decided not to bugger off to the hospital until I'd finished making the tea. Nearly dropped me load stirring the bloody potatoes. Just made it to the labour ward. Can take you by surprise, babies."

It was Saturday. George was about to be christened.

Exactly why George was about to be christened nobody could have said. It had seemed to his mother and guardians like a good idea, agnostics though they were. It had seemed like an appropriate way to offset the informality of George's birth, to take him all dressed up in the family christening gown down to the village church and have him done – as if the holy water and the solemn ritual could somehow restore his prestige, or even bestow upon him a hint of legitimacy. In any case, it had been arranged.

It was a hot afternoon. There had been little rain for several weeks and the plants in the garden were yellowing, as were the thistles in the field, golden, spiky and gleaming. After the ceremony there was to be a picnic tea in the garden which was to be shared by Pat and Gill, Bob from the hostel in which Judith had lived for a time after she left her house in Mackworth Street, and several of the friends she had made while she was there, including Dora, Herbert, Pansy, Maureen and Arthur. They were all to be present at the ceremony and then to partake of the large quantities of food which Judith, Susannah, Helen and Pat had prepared, and to drink the even greater abundance of wine provided by Hector.

As well as elevating George, the christening would be a milestone along the roadside of Hector and Judith's marriage. It would be an occasion. It would be a tribute to the children which Hector and Judith could never have. It would be a party. It would be a salute and a benediction.

Judith and Hector and Bob were to be George's godparents, as they had all been through the church's portals during childhood and were deemed fit to undertake these duties. And Susannah, who had never been in a church in her life, by virtue of the fact that she was desperate to be attached formally to this baby, was to be his honorary godmother – the vicar having had several talks with her and assured himself of her earnest wish to become better acquainted with the Church's teaching in order to steer George in the right direction through the course of his life.

Susannah thought the whole thing was a load of old cod's bollocks. But so anxious was she to belong to this baby which she had caught as he was born that she allowed herself to undergo the formalities of religion in much the same way that she had allowed herself to be subjected to ECT. Later, she would allow herself to be baptised and confirmed in order to be fit to take care of George. And she was sure that, as in the case of the ECT, these procedures would not greatly alter her view of life. There would be no blinding flash on the road to Damascus for Susannah. Yet she had a curious feeling that *something* would happen. In all his conversations with her the vicar had addressed her as somebody with an identity of her own – an identity which not only gave her a soul, whatever that was, but also made her fit to care for another soul. In this religion was greatly superior to ECT which dealt with everyone in the same way and was absolutely no respecter or aggrandiser of persons.

"Shall we stir them up a bit? Time's going on," said Pat.

"Little bugger has probably vomited all over the christening gown," Gill suggested helpfully. "Couldn't blame him. Must be tough for a good butch Australian being buttoned into yards and yards of lace."

"He's not crying," Judith pointed out. "It'll be Susannah, fussing about getting everything right. She won't allow him to have an uncomfortable wrinkle or fold anywhere."

"What about his Mum? Doesn't she see to him?" Pat was ready to be indignant. "It's all very well being progressive and emancipated but you can't just have a baby casually like that, as if it was a night out at Bingo, and then detach yourself as if it had happened to somebody else."

"They do though, you know." Gill was serious. "They forget about them. Around our way they go straight back to work and palm it off on anybody that will have it."

Judith wished that this subject had not arisen. It saddened her to be reminded that Helen allowed Susannah to mother the baby. Obviously it was good for Susannah, and George was thriving. But it seemed so unnatural. She knew very well that upstairs Helen would be reading a book – her clothing immaculate, her hair gleaming, her nails scarlet – and that Susannah would be cradling George, her own appearance as yet unconsidered. And Hector would soon be back from helping to take the hostel crowd to the church, there not having been enough room for them all in Bob's car.

She went to the foot of the stairs.

"Helen. Susannah," she called. "Are you ready? Hector will be back in a few minutes."

It was ironic. Some people drifted through their days as the thistleheads drift across the fields, hardly touching anything yet apparently covering vast spaces, while others seemed to become entangled in every possible obstacle, as though for them any sort of progress were an utter impossibility. Judith sympathised with people who found things difficult. After all, she was one of them. But she felt that there was still a purpose, a destiny for those whose paths are obstructed. Helen didn't appear to possess the family steadfastness. But Susannah, who had nothing to do with the family, did.

These thoughts persisted in her mind as she stood by the font with Helen and her great-nephew, his dark curly head ridiculously rich against the yellowing lace of the ancient christening robe. Sarah had entrusted this to Judith before she died. It was a symbol of baptism. Although Sarah's religion was not conventional, baptism had been an important, as well as a frequent, experience in her life. For Sarah baptism had held the same significance that George's ad hoc family hoped to find in today's ceremony; it represented some kind of putting in order. Sarah's life, like George's, had lacked a certain cohesion.

Susannah stood next to Hector. The Vicar accepted George from his mother and a little murmur of wondering admiration passed between Dora, Herbert, Maureen, Arthur and Pansy as he gave the clerical gentleman an engaging smile.

"Eh, in't he bonny? We'll have one like that one day," said Maureen to Arthur, who nudged her reprovingly with his elbow and looked bashful. They had been married for a year and were managing exceedingly well in a supervised house close to the hostel with two other couples.

"Wind," said Pansy, sniffing into a tidy handkerchief. "Ought to have given him some gripe water afore they started." She was wondering who polished the pews, and what they used on them. They'd got a grand shine.

Dora was shedding a tear. Babies always made her cry.

Herbert adjusted his teeth as the water dropped on to George's forehead. He looked thoughtfully up at the roof of the church, wondering where the bells were kept.

Susannah, feeling Hector's arm against hers, was in another world. Once again she felt as if she were flying. She was elevated by the quiet words, the comfort of these people gathered for the obscure purpose of giving something to George. She was not quite sure what they were giving to him. But she was glad. Perhaps whatever it was would keep him safe. Susannah felt a current of air gently carrying her forwards and sideways. She felt herself flying, and Hector, glancing down at her wrapt face below the straw hat, was moved as he had not been moved before. He held her elbow lightly as the time came for their participation and heard her make the response in a quiet, resolute voice.

Afterwards they all made merry. Gill, standing on a chair in the centre of the rose bed, did her impersonation of Gracie Fields, using an empty beer bottle as a microphone. Herbert wore a policeman's helmet which Judith had borrowed for the occasion from the local constabulary. Pansy recited Wordsworth's Daffodils. Maureen and Arthur sang 'You'll Never Walk Alone' and with the record player turned on full blast in the kitchen Hector and Dora gave a demonstration of the tango on the terrace which was filled with as much dramatic emphasis as it was devoid of finesse. Pat had taken over the dispensing of the comestibles, pressing everyone to more, and gathering in anyone who seemed shy or unable to care for themselves, while Bob, himself becoming very convivial, dispensed the imbibables.

"Jesus," thought Helen admiringly, as her son was passed from hand to hand beaming with that particularly delightful if somewhat stupid expression which babies adopt when they are storing up attention for the future development of enormous egos, "Jesus, they're all screwy. But they're doing us proud."

George, exhausted at last by his role as the star of the show, was fed and put into his cot to sleep it off.

His cot had long ago been installed in Susannah's attic bedroom so that Helen, who had complained bitterly after his birth, could rest undisturbed.

36

Hector woke up.

Judith, for once, was sleeping soundly, lying on her stomach, her face pressed into the pillow as if she were a bee searching for honey in the sepals of a deep flower, her hand curled beside her mouth.

For a moment he could not decide what had woken him. It was dark, but the edges of the curtains were tinged with the beginnings of the morning. Then he felt Susannah's hand on his shoulder. She was carrying George in her arms.

Hector slid out of bed and hurried Susannah out of the bedroom, closing the door quietly behind them. The landing light was on.

George was choking. His face was blue and there were dark marks under his eyes. Susannah was white and silent.

Hector seized George and holding him upside down administered a smart thump with his fist to the triangle between the baby's little shoulder blades.

George coughed and a small lump of mucus shot out of his mouth. He took a desperate draught of air and began to breathe rapid shallow breaths. Hector righted him and examined his face. His colour had begun to return and he opened his mouth until it seemed to occupy the whole of his head, screwing up his eyes as if he wanted to cry but not making any noise. The smudges under his eyes remained, purplish and shiny.

Hector handed George back to Susannah as he began to whimper, a croaky, dry parody of his usual lusty yell.

"Take him back upstairs. I'll go and get a teaspoon to have a look at his throat."

Susannah's eyes were full of tears. She clutched George

to her thin bosom and climbed back to her attic bedroom.

When Hector returned she was rocking the child, which having discovered that it was painful and difficult to cry, had closed its eyes and lay resigned and waiting, like an old man about to die.

"What can be the matter with him? He was fine when I put him to bed. Then he started making funny noises. It woke me up. Is it my fault? What have I done to him?"

Hector was examining George's throat, peering through his spectacles, feeling the sides of his neck, the glands under his chin, with gentle, capable fingers.

"He'll be OK, Susannah. His throat is a bit inflamed. Babies are like that. One minute they are in rude health and the next minute they are putting everybody into a fine state of panic. Go and get him a drink of warm water. Put a little honey into it. We'll see how he is in the morning. He could be perfectly all right in a couple of hours." He looked at Susannah, pale as a dried bulrush leaf, and smiled his wide smile. "And it's certainly not anything that you've done to him, my dear. You've just got him out of a nasty fix. Go on, get him a drink. I won't leave him. And for heaven's sake, don't make a noise. We don't want to disturb Judith. She has to get up early for work."

Susannah was crying properly as she hurried back down the attic stairs, holding on to the banister rail firmly to guide herself because she couldn't see through her tears. As she passed the door of Helen's room she heard the Australian girl snoring.

"Bloody woman," she thought, feeling her normal personality taking over again. "Bloody woman. George could have been dead." And as she prepared the baby's drink she found that she was crying for other reasons.

She was crying for Gavin who was dead.

Hector replaced George in his cot and looked around Susannah's bedroom. It was filled with the treasures that she had amassed since she left the hospital, a brass camel that Judith had bought for her at the flea market, a Victorian needlepoint posy of flowers which she had paid for in instalments out of her dole money at a junk shop, curtains with a delicate pattern of leaves which she had chosen and insisted on buying for herself, the bird mobile which she had taken back from Helen's bedroom and suspended from the beam over George's cot. He watched the paper birds, painted in bright colours, revolving slowly in the warmth of the light bulb, dancing a minuet, interweaving and circling with eighteenth-century grace.

A great sense of wonder stole through his consciousness. This was the inside of Susannah. This was what had been hiding under the hostility, the despair. All that craziness had been an expression of the frustration of this appreciation of peace and order. All that suffering had come directly from this centre of herself, like the pearly centre of a shell on a shifting beach which had been filled with the merciless crashing of pebbles flung into it over and over again by a heedless sea.

"A spiritual disease," he thought suddenly. "Not a mental illness but a spiritual one. A defence against the invasion of the soul. Perhaps that's what's wrong with all of us."

He heard her coming quietly back up the stairs and felt a terrible sense of humility. Humility and love.

37

In the morning George was not better.

"What's the matter with you, petal?" asked Tulip as Judith settled herself at her table and began, numbly, to pack free bags for powder compacts into envelopes addressed with sticky labels to various parts of the country. "I think these are pretty, don't you? Don't care for the pink ones. But the purple ones are a dream. I'd like a bra made out of this purple stuff. That'd do something for my appeal. They'd all come running if I had a bra made out of this purple stuff. And pants, of course. Briefs. Two compact bags for the bra, one for each boob, and about five for the pants, two for the back and three for the front. Do you think Ma Eccles would notice if I half-inched a few? Come on, cheer up. You look like you'd just lost your virginity."

"It's the baby. He's ill. The doctor is coming to see him this morning. I would have liked to be there. They are so young, those two girls. I should have been there to help them."

Susan, who had been listening, turned round and gave Judith a mocking grin.

"Your Helen and Susannah are a lot older than I was. I managed all right. Babies are up and down, or rather down and up, in no time. What's the betting when you get home at tea-time he'll be his usual cheeky self."

"Do you think so?" Judith stretched a rubber band around a bundle of fat envelopes and stacked it against the others. If only she could stop the anxiety which assailed her like the insistent ringing of a telephone. When she had looked forward to having the baby she had forgotten all this, the dry terror of nights when they were ill, the panicky walking up and down, the urge to run outside and run and run and run until it was all far behind.

"Course I do. My Nicola used to scare the shit out of me one minute. The next she was pushing buses over."

The young have such elasticity. They are not persecuted by dark fears. They do not live on the brink of disaster. They swim confidently from one day to the next like sure swimmers exploring safe water.

At least, some of them do.

Helen had not been in the least perturbed at breakfast.

"Has it got a cold then, the poor old Georgie?" she had crooned, bouncing the sick baby so that his head wobbled and Susannah winced.

But Helen did not have the practical skills which should accompany this kind of confidence. And Susannah, who had the practical skills, like Judith and unlike Helen, also had the unreasonable, blind agitation.

Not for the first time Judith felt that she could not cope with her job and her domestic life. She should have been there when the doctor came. They might forget to tell him something important. Helen might so easily spend his visit playing the serene mother and humiliating Susannah in the process. She should have been there to make sure that everything was done properly – that Helen did not upset Susannah, that George did not become either the victim of Susannah's paralysed terror or of Helen's thick-skinned unconcern.

She would have a word with Mrs Eccles. After being at the packaging firm for over two years she thought that she might be allowed to leave for a time – perhaps until Helen and the baby went back to Australia, when although her heart would bleed the problem would no longer be hers. She knew that Hector would be quite happy for her to give up her job. She had kept it since her marriage out of a sense of pride and because she did not wish to burden him financially, though she knew that he was well able to support her and would be glad to have her constantly at home.

She would do it. At lunch-time she would catch Mrs Eccles

before the women began to clatter down the shallow wooden stairs and tell her that she intended to leave. If she could not have her job back when the time came she would have to think again. But in the meanwhile she would act decisively.

Tulip was counting her compact bags, piling them in piles of ten which fell one by one to the splintery floor.

"Damn things. I seem to have lost about half-a-dozen," she muttered, crawling about under her table. "That puts paid to the bra and panties project. The old buzzard would certainly notice if there were twelve missing."

38

To say that Hector was troubled would be an understatement.

How could he, how could he feel the way he did?

Judith. My lovely Judith.

He thought about her vulnerability. He thought about her trust. He thought about her strange, half-mad affinity with things that she touched and her dependence on people's goodwill.

And the more he thought about her, about the new understanding she had inadvertently given him of his own life, and indeed of the lives of others, the more miserable he became. For he knew that the very existence of Susannah jeopardised everything they had created between them.

Oh, for God's sake, why? What is the danger? What is being endangered? Judith knows that I need her. She knows that no volatile, disturbed girl is going to threaten our happiness. She knows that we are together and real in a way that circumstances cannot alter.

But was Susannah 'circumstances'?

At what stage did the presence of an attractive and passionate young woman in the attic, who needed support and comfort in order to ensure that she would at some time find a stable and enduring happiness of her own, at what stage did this dangerous presence become 'circumstances'? Moreover, could this person find anyone else but himself to supply her needs?

Hector knew, perhaps wrongly, that he was not unique. But he also knew that his new relationship with Susannah was as unique as that with his wife.

It was not a question of morality or even of professional ethics.

It was a practical problem.

He did not know either how to contain or how to express his deep feeling for two women, both of whom needed him, and were needed by him, completely.

39

Mrs Eccles was not pleased.

"Well, you know, dear, there are always people looking for jobs. You can get in touch with me when you feel you would like to come back. But I can't guarantee anything. You'll have to chance it. If there's a place there's a place. If not I shan't be able to help you." She looked down at Judith, trying to assess this worker, trying to evaluate her contribution to the smooth running of the department.

She found that she could remember nothing about her. Most of the women were either tiresomely inefficient, like Tulip, whose work always had to be done again, or they worked swiftly and neatly and could be relied upon to do what they were told and make a good job of it. Mrs Eccles had to tolerate the Tulips of this world. But they were greatly outnumbered by workers like young Sylvia who never put a foot wrong. Judith wasn't either inefficient like Tulip or speedy and capable like Sylvia. She was not remarkable in any way. There was nothing about her that would be remembered the week after next.

Mrs Eccles believed in encouraging her workers to stay for as long as possible. It lent an air of continuity to the department. New people had to be instructed and their habits studied. Judith hadn't any habits. She always arrived on time. She had made friends with a small number of the other women and some of the lads. But she was not one of those who were inclined to talk constantly. In fact, she wasn't one of those about whom there was anything either praiseworthy or irritating to record.

It was irritating, though, that she was leaving.

Mrs Eccles was a tidy person. Replacing workers led to

untidiness. Judith's replacement might be another Tulip.

Or she might be a Sylvia. Mrs Eccles brightened up.

"Well, I hope you'll enjoy being at home with your family," she added wondering what a woman of Judith's age was doing with a family which still lived with her, "and as I say, if you want to come back you can get in touch."

Walking to the bus stop with Tulip at the end of the day Judith felt a mixture of relief and regret. Like many Lancashire women she did not believe that she was fully herself if she had no job. And yet, and yet. The prospect of having all her days to enjoy the cottage and the garden and Hector and the baby filled her with a sense of exhilaration. She knew that she would not be bored for a second. She knew that she would not be lonely without her working friends. Helen, in spite of her shortcomings as a mother, was entertaining. And with Susannah about life was never dull.

A car drew up beside them. It contained a large bearded Asian gentleman and three younger unbearded Asian gentlemen. The bearded gentleman leaned out of the open window and gave Tulip a thoughtful stare. Tulip, clad in a sea-green sari and orange trousers, her sandal straps loose around her bare feet, turned a deep shade of crimson and muttered,

"Bloody men."

Judith put her arm through Tulip's and they hurried up the hill towards the bus stop.

"They think if they see an Asian woman in the street that she is anybody's," Tulip explained, turning around and scowling at the car which was cruising along just behind them. "Thank God I was with you. That should put them off."

Judith felt that there might have been something a shade uncomplimentary about Tulip's last remark, but she couldn't put her finger on what it was.

"Well, I hope you'll be able to manage without me," she said earnestly as they reached the place at which their routes diverged.

Tulip looked at her seriously, the jewel in the side of her nostril glittering like a star in the late afternoon sunlight.

"I'll miss you, Judy," she said, and hesitated. The car sped past them up the road, its heavy, silent occupants staring grimly ahead.

"I'd be very glad if you'd come to visit me," Judith said. "I think you'd like our cottage, and the baby and everything."

Tulip's face lit up.

"I'll come on a Saturday," she replied. "I know which bus to catch. That'd be grand. It gets boring, Saturdays."

Judith watched her friend swinging on up the hill. It was not surprising that Tulip was troubled by men. She had a certain air, a certain exotic appeal, like the appeal of a rare, gloriously scented flower opening its petals in the bright light and abandoning itself to the pleasurable promises of nature. It would be nice to entertain Tulip in the village. Judith didn't suppose that Tulip had ever seen much of the Lancashire countryside, brought up in the backstreets of an industrial community from which even the industry which had given it its character was gradually being lost.

She put the thought of work out of her mind and began to worry about George as she settled herself on the bus.

40

During George's illness which lasted for several days Hector became accustomed to climbing the attic stairs at bedtime with Susannah to inspect the baby before they all retired for the night.

He found himself, during these few days, thinking increasingly about the visit to the attic as he toured the hospital wards and dealt with patients in his clinic. He found himself thinking of it with a strange lifting of his spirits, as a schoolboy during his Latin lesson thinks about football, frog-spawn, and ice-cream. The more he thought about these visits, the more he realised that the dangerous feelings they gave him were not reasonable and might destroy the whole precious structure of his existence.

He knew himself very well. He was accustomed to reviewing the state of his mind and adjusting his responses in order to fit in with other people and prevailing circumstances. He also knew Susannah very well, and he knew that she, too, with her new self-awareness, was trying to adapt. Neither of them wished to smash the status quo. Neither of them wished to fluster Judith, who now that she was no longer hurrying off to work each morning had more time to observe them both.

Hector experienced a familiar kind of despair.

Surrounded as he was and had always been by human suffering he tended to feel, as indeed he often advised his patients, that within obvious limits it was sensible to take any road which made living positive instead of negative. The difficulty arose when this road conflicted with other roads, when, in fact, one came to a crossroads. He knew that he was now at a crossroads. He knew that his desire to comfort

Susannah as an expression of his wish to comfort the whole of humankind had turned into quite a different kind of desire, and he could tell by Susannah's deliberate detachment from him that for the first time in her life she, too, was considering the possible consequences of taking a course she wanted to take and checking her own will by going an alternative route.

Should he examine George before Susannah took him upstairs to bed?

No, he thought; on the whole it was better if he saw him later on, just to satisfy himself that the child was breathing well and was still on the mend.

So he climbed the stairs, watching Susannah's brown legs ascending in front of him. He tiptoed across the pale tufted carpet and removed the cotton blanket which covered George. Susannah and Judith had made the blanket, patching together a rainbow of coloured bits which provided a hazy panorama which the baby loved.

George was sleeping peacefully.

Hector placed the palm of his hand across the baby's forehead and smiled contentedly. Susannah was looking at him, not at George. She knew that George was all right. She had known for two days. But having Hector in her bedroom gave her a curious feeling of serenity which lasted through the night. It was as if the few minutes that he spent there cast a glow which persisted after he had gone, as the evening sky holds the tones of the sunset long after the sun has disappeared. She could not have described this feeling. Happiness was still too new an experience for her to be able to associate it with times gone by. It had begun with the moments in which she had felt as if she were flying. It had returned, spasmodically, in unforeseen, split-second recognitions, vanishing as swiftly as it came. But recently it had remained for longer and longer intervals – a sense of well-being, a sense of peace. She knew that, although she loved the baby and found consolation in looking after him, although she loved Judith and found pleasure in trying to please her, although she had come to like Helen, and was grateful to her for not wanting her own child, although she enjoyed living in a proper home and found the quiet soothing and healing, she knew that in spite of all these things it was Hector and Hector alone who had introduced her to this unfamiliar state of mind.

And she was desperate to conceal it. She was conscious as she surveyed her image in the oak-framed mirror in her bedroom that she was now a different person, a different woman, a real woman. She knew that she had a kind of beauty which Judith had not and would never have. She knew that Hector had noticed it.

He had gone downstairs again, touching her shoulder and saying, as he had said every night,

"I'm sure he's fine now. But don't lie and worry about him. If you have any doubts come down and wake me up."

She leaned out of the window, high above Cecil's trees, high above the geraniums and the little lawn and Judith's beloved shrubs and plants and stared into the sky. She observed a small red light which was followed as if from afar by the faint sound of an aeroplane engine. For an absurd moment she thought the red light of the aeroplane was standing still in the heavens with all those multitudes of stars crashing past it at great speed as the sparkling ocean crashes past the hull of a motor-boat.

"Oh God," thought Susannah. "What the hell am I going to do now?"

41

But it was not in response to an appeal from Susannah for help with the baby that, finally, Hector climbed quietly up the attic stairs and inflamed the malady of his conscience while relieving the human ache in his soul.

And Judith, waking at three o'clock in the morning, heard the faint sound of Hector's special voice from the room above, the faint sound of movement in Susannah's bed, the faint sound of inconceivable bliss in Susannah's barely audible tones.

Before she was sufficiently awake to register the fact that she was alone in the bed she realised that she was not alone.

There beside her was the unmistakable shape of her husband, Murphy.

Judith was very upset. She knew that Hector was making love to Susannah. But she also knew that if she woke Murphy to tell him, he would be very angry. Murphy hated to be woken during the night. Once she had gone downstairs during one of her monitoring tours of the household. Maria had dropped a tumbler at supper-time and prowling about in her bare feet Judith had stepped on a small piece of glass which had been overlooked during the sweeping-up process. Her foot had begun to bleed profusely and she had run upstairs to Murphy crying with fear, trying to staunch the flow of blood with a tea-towel.

"Murphy, I've cut my foot," she exclaimed, shaking his heavy arm.

Murphy turned over and chewed noisily a few times as if trying out a new kind of food.

"Murphy, Murphy, wake up, I'm bleeding to death," she implored.

Murphy, realising that he was going to have to say something, advised her companionably, "OK but do it quietly," before rolling over and going back to sleep.

No. It was no use. She mustn't wake Murphy. It always put him into such a bad mood. He would be impossible in the morning if she disturbed him to tell him that Hector was up in the attic making love to Susannah.

It was no use. She lay trying not to listen to the hushed communications from above. Perhaps she should go downstairs. But if she went downstairs Murphy might wake up and shout at her. She would have to stay where she was.

She began to feel confused.

Murphy started to snore. Though she had not slept with Murphy for so long, instinctively she heaved with her shoulder to get him over on to his side. This sometimes caused the snoring to diminish.

The snoring might wake Helen.

Or it might disturb Hector.

What would Hector think if he came down from the attic and found Murphy in his side of the bed?

After all, he was her husband.

Who was her husband?

Hector was her husband. Yes, but so was Murphy. Murphy had been her husband before Hector was. It was strange, wasn't it, that when Murphy left her to go and live with his Susy she had felt no jealousy, no real sorrow. But then she had had Hector. Now that Hector had gone to Susannah, she had nobody.

Of course she had somebody. She had Murphy. What, then, had happened to Murphy's Susy? Perhaps he had grown tired of her. Men often went off with young, beautiful women then tired of them and came back to their uninteresting, devoted wives. Susannah was young and beautiful, with her gleaming hair and her clear skin and those intense, fathomless blue eyes. Perhaps Hector would tire of Susannah and come back to her. But Murphy was here in any case. Though she didn't think she could manage them both, if

Hector returned. Not any more, when she and Hector had been so much one person, so whole.

Judith began to cry, very quietly, lying on her stomach with her face pressed against her pillow, conscious that she must not waken Murphy. He was now lying with his back to her, no longer snoring but breathing deeply, making a noise like the purring of a cat that has always been well-cared for. She knew that she did not belong to anybody, that nobody belonged to her. She knew that she had never belonged to anybody. Although Murphy had always looked after her and been kind to her in his own way, he had never been an integral part of herself. And Hector, who had seemed like the unexpressed, deepest essence of herself, Hector had always been like the magical prince in the pantomime, a prince dressed up as an ordinary person dressed up as a prince. But he must have been an ordinary person after all. She had always suspected that following him into the enchanted forest would end like this. She was alone in territory which she could not cope with alone. She had been living in a fantasy. She had given herself up entirely to the charms of this forest which had lured her on, day after day, with its endless delights. Now she was far into its darkness and she did not know which way to plunge through the undergrowth to find sunlight on the other side. Nor could she go back. The way back was overgrown with giant rose trees, vermilion lilies, gemlike mosses which would catch her feet and cause her to stumble and fall with every step.

There was no way forward. And there was no way back.

As the sun began to lighten the contours of the hill, still anxious to conceal her grief from Murphy for fear of annoying him, she fell into a disturbed sleep, so that Hector, when he climbed back into his side of the bed feeling like a prince, knew that so far everything was all right. He would just have to play it by ear, one day at a time.

But his conscience, as he leaned across and kissed the top of Judith's silver head, cried out in agony.

42

Helen could not understand it. As a reporter she had always considered herself a fairly worldly and tolerant individual, mature for her years and able to judge people and events from unusual points of view.

When she had arrived in Farringham she had not been surprised by what she at once recognised as an aberrant menage in which her aunt seemed little more unusual than the rest. As a child Helen had often heard her father talk affectionately about his older sister who though odd had obviously done so much to ensure that he and his siblings grew up at all, let alone grew up properly. She had, therefore, been prepared for a certain degree of eccentricity in her aunt. She had not, however, realised that the entire household would be eccentric. Judith had told her in a letter, for instance, that she and Hector had living with them a dear young girl who suffered from great misfortune and needed all their love and understanding. But Judith had not told her, and Helen had only just realised, that there was an interesting relationship between this dear young girl and Judith's husband, Hector. Helen had not been prepared for this phenomenon. Nor had it dawned on her, and she chided herself for her lack of perception, that the phenomenon existed, until this morning.

There could be no question about it at all. Susannah's truculence towards her benefactor, her rudeness and ill-temper, and his amused rejoinders had thrown the young woman completely. It had not entered her mind that these evidences of camaraderie were deliberately planted by the pair in order to disguise the fact that they were lovers.

This morning, though, at breakfast, it all became very

clear. This morning there was no disguising the fact that Hector and Susannah were lovers; no amount of repartee, no apparent indifference on Susannah's part and paternal leg-pulling on Hector's could hide Susannah's soft mystery and Hector's masculine pride.

And Aunt Judith. For God's sake, what had happened to Aunt Judith? She suddenly looked about ninety, drawn around the eyes, lined where even her lined face had not been lined before, pale under her sunburn, her silver hair in disarray, her expression weird and abstracted, as if as she listened to the general conversation she were also attending to an insistent conversation of her own and joining in the two conversations at one and the same time. Even her voice had changed. The sonorous quality had gone from it as the wholesome sound of a good bell vanishes when it is cracked.

Hector, preparing to leave for the hospital, was beside himself. He couldn't take his eyes away from the vision that was Susannah, spooning egg into George who sat with his head back and his mouth open like a fledgling, her face bright and her body appearing rounder and more liberal than it usually did. She was not actually singing a little song, but somehow she gave the impression that she had become one, a clear, lilting melody, a warm, earthy lyric, a delicate medley of words and music.

What, though, had happened to Judith?

He examined her carefully.

She had been deeply asleep when he had left her and she had been deeply asleep when he returned to bed. No doubt about that. She could not possibly have been aware that he had crept up the attic stairs. He was sufficiently in touch with his motives, even at this moment, to realise that the danger of wakening her had added to his excitement. But she could not have heard.

Or could she?

She had not been pretending to sleep. He was sure of that. He had slept too long with her watchful wakefulness not to recognise her sound slumber when it came to pass. And surely, if she had woken and found him absent she would have got up and looked for him.

No. It must be something else. Something had upset her. But it was not anything that he had done. She had the distracted look which came over her when she was troubled by one of her obscure anxieties. He decided that the best way to deal with it was to behave as if it was not there. Since she had stopped working he had been coming home for a quick lunch. He would see how she seemed at lunchtime, and if necessary revise his opinion.

Meanwhile he must try to treat Susannah as if the earth had not moved.

That was going to be difficult.

Susannah did not find it difficult to treat Hector as if the earth had not moved. For her the earth had not moved. For her today was just like yesterday, except that she was tired, not having had her eight hours' sleep.

It wasn't that she hadn't been overjoyed when Hector woke her. It wasn't that making love with Hector hadn't been a new experience, quite unlike any experience of making love that she had ever had before. It wasn't that, this morning, she didn't feel more feminine, more luxuriant, more vivid than she had felt in her life.

It was just that all this did not solve the problem. In fact, it exacerbated the problem exceedingly. She was now the mistress of the husband of a woman who had been kinder and more understanding than anyone had ever been to her, and she had become his mistress in this gentle person's own home.

For Susannah considerations of this nature were also a new experience. She had never felt it necessary to imagine how other people might be affected by her actions, unless it was in order to make them more efficiently destructive.

But watching Judith, who was usually so deft, fumbling with everyday objects, fumbling with words, fumbling her way through the early morning appalled Susannah. No such practical assessments as Hector's passed through her consciousness. For Susannah, whether Judith could possibly have known what was happening in the attic seemed irrelevant. For Susannah there was a straight line running from what she had done to the state in which she now found Judith. The line was as direct as that grim parade of diminishing trees.

For Susannah and Hector alike there had arisen a terrible storm, like a storm in an orchard at blossom time. In each of them blew fierce winds of guilt and regret, there blazed flashes of fearful lightning, there crashed the awful sounds of thunder, while in each of them also the white, fragrant petals touched and smothered them with the unutterable delight of being in love.

They both knew that they had done something foolish, hazardous and wrong.

But what else could they have done?

43

Alas, poor Judith.

By lunchtime Hector knew that she was as ill as she had ever been. She was not suicidal, but she was no longer living in the same world as everyone else. She was back, once more, in the dungeon of her deluded imagination. He also knew that she had woken during the night, found him absent and not looked for him but listened to the whisperings from the attic which told her that she had again been hurled into a situation with which she could not cope.

"Murphy says will you please stay up there, Hector," she said when he arrived home for his sandwich. "I know it's a lot to ask, and I don't really like asking you. He does get so annoyed about things which don't fit in with his way of life. You know how it is." She smiled apologetically at Hector, hoping that he would not make a fuss, dreading the confrontation which would surely take place between the two men when Murphy came in from work. If only Hector would just go to the attic it would save a dreadful scene.

Her eyes seemed to have grown deeper and clear, hauntingly clear, like sea water through which, in the bright light, you can see shapes of monsters threatening tragedy as they lurk amongst the rocks below.

"My love, why should I stay in the attic?" Hector protested, feeling these monsters already gnawing at his soul.

"Because, of course," Judith explained, "we can't all three fit in the same bed. And Murphy works hard. He deserves and needs a good night's sleep."

"Who is Murphy?" Helen asked, astonished. What the bloody hell was going on here?

Susannah was sitting by the table in the kitchen holding

George on her knee. She scraped the surplus apple pudding from a teaspoon and inserted the rest between the baby's co-operative lips. George grabbed the teaspoon and while Susannah was attempting to retrieve it and most of the apple pudding was leaking back out through his grin he managed to poke Susannah in the eye with it.

"Oh George," moaned Susannah, "let me have the teaspoon. You know you like pudding. Eat it up like a good boy." If it had been this time yesterday they would all have laughed. Today, it seemed as if the baby were deliberately complicating a stalemate so complete that nobody could move a step in any direction.

Judith turned tensely towards Helen and said,

"Murphy's come back. I knew he would. I always knew that it couldn't last. She never understood him as I did. I mean, after all those years together. You start knowing what the other person is going to say before they say it. It's always the same. They think there is something missing but they don't know what it is. They go off in search of it and think they have found it. But sooner or later they realise that they haven't. Then they either go further and further like somebody lost in the mountains, just climbing one more peak, or else, if they haven't gone too far they come home. Murphy has always been the sort who came home." She turned from Helen to Hector and added, her eyes full of tears,

"I'm awfully sorry, Hector. I should have known this would happen. We can still be friends, can't we? He probably won't make too much fuss as long as we look after him properly."

"Look," demanded Helen, growing angry, "what is going on? Have I been left out of something? I mean, I know I'm only the nuisance niece from Australia, but I think in view of that fact that I'm living here for the present I should be put in the picture. I know this house has harboured a lot of people on occasions but it seems to me that if somebody else has arrived George and I should move on. You can have my room and then nobody needs to be put out. I should be going home, in any case. I can't stay here forever. And George is huge I shan't be able to carry him if he gets much bigger."

Susannah felt a cold band around her chest, like a strip of icy metal. She drew George closer to her and ladled the apple pudding carefully into his mouth, trying to control the trembling of the teaspoon.

Hector took Judith's hands in his and struggled with a hundred conflicting emotions. Out of his difficulty in knowing where to start explaining to Helen what had happened, his quiet joy in the presence of Susannah, his agitation about her distress at the thought of losing the baby, his horror and guilt and anxiety in the face of what he had done to his wife and his general, universally profound sorrow before the sickness of humankind, he chose to express his love for Judith.

"Darling," he said in a stricken voice, "you and I know all about Murphy, don't we? We know that Murphy is not going to come between us. We know that we can cope with Murphy. We've coped with him before. It's all of us against Murphy. There's no way he's going to turn the clock back. You and I are married."

"I know that, Hector. But it just makes me feel worse. I should have stayed as I was and waited for him. After all, I love him. And you were managing your life all right. Murphy needed me. I shouldn't have left him. We have a lot in common, Murphy and I, all those years, all those children, all those brushes with death."

"But what about us? What about what we've got, what we've had? What about our happiness? Have you forgotten that?" Hector, in his desperation, had begun to forget what it was all about. With the penetrating directness of the crazy Judith reminded him.

"Then why did you go to Susannah last night?" she asked.

Susannah burst into tears and ran out of the kitchen, George in her arms clutching at her hair with rage and surprise as she divorced him from the remains of his apple pudding.

Helen was sitting with her mouth open.

Now that Susannah was no longer present Hector found

his problems had diminished very slightly, as the contents of a reservoir might be said to have increased by the occurrence of one short shower of rain during a particularly severe drought.

"I went to Susannah last night because I love her. Just as you love both me and Murphy so I love both you and Susannah. Because I love Susannah as well as you doesn't mean that I love you any less. I love you and need you, as I've always loved and needed you. But I also love Susannah, and I need her, too."

Judith looked carefully at Hector. She felt very sorry for him. He appeared lost in a way that she had never seen him lost before. Somewhere, as if from far away, she seemed to understand what he was saying. It was as if somewhere, perhaps in some other existence, this had all happened to her before, this tempest of contradictory emotions, this abyss of fear and sadness, this sense that she was being dragged in one direction by one arm and in the other direction by the other with no choice about which way she went, simply suffering the central pain of being torn apart. Then she remembered.

She remembered her days in the clothing factory when she had been made to choose between her love for Hector and her love for Murphy. She had chosen Hector. This had obviously been a wrong choice. Murphy now needed her again. She should have foreseen that. She should have arranged things somehow so that she could remain with them both. She suddenly saw the logic of Hector's explanation. Of course. That was it. That was the answer. Last time, when she was trying to make up her mind, Hector had somehow managed to persuade her to leave Murphy. She shouldn't have done it. It was all clear in her mind now. Just as Hector loved and needed both her and Susannah, so she, Judith, loved and needed both Hector and Murphy. That was the answer.

"OK, Hector," she said earnestly. "Don't worry about it. We'll work it out. We'll all live together."

44

"I've explained as well as I can. I knew, I did know, what might happen. I shall not forget what she was like years ago. But you must understand my position." Hector was trying to light his pipe, miserably stuffing the tobacco down into it and applying one match after another as if it was the cause of his woes and if he could succeed in persuading it to burn they would be disposed of, like the garden rubbish in a bonfire.

"Oh, don't bother trying to explain it to me. I know all about men. Aunt Judith's quite right about that. They always think there's something missing, behave badly but still expect everyone who is involved with them to be overwhelmed with love and gratitude."

Having recovered from the lunchtime trauma, Helen, now that she had some of the facts at her disposal, found herself in a mood of unforgiving disbelief. Susannah had taken Judith upstairs and the two were temporarily oblivious of the smoulderings left by the storm, mutually absorbed as they both were in a fine entertainment being provided by George, the central character in his ritual bathing ceremony.

"Judith is a schizoid depressive," Hector said firmly. "Judith, having been my patient, became my wife."

"Well, you bloody well married her. She wasn't forced on you by the authorities."

"Let me finish. Of course I married her. I married her because I loved her, because I love her. But you must realise that to live one's whole life with somebody who has been one's patient imposes a great strain."

"So you set about having it off with another patient in order to relieve the tension."

"For two and a half years I have carefully avoided any

situation which I considered might threaten her stability."

"And now you've changed your tactics and plunged straight into one which you could fully guarantee would make her nuts."

"I can understand that as Judith's niece you feel you must disregard my point of view. Nevertheless I have one."

"Of course. Every sodding man on the planet has a point of view. And they are all orientated towards diminishing the female."

"Helen, I have never wished to diminish anyone. I spend my days endeavouring to shore up and support people who have been seriously damaged, many of them beyond repair. Judith was one who had been more seriously damaged than most. I undertook to help her to become as whole as was possible and ultimately, to live with and enjoy the fruits of my labours."

"Exactly. You married her out of vanity and as soon as the bloom had worn off you began to look around for more excitement."

"That is not so."

"Then why did you allow yourself to get involved with Susannah?"

"Susannah had nobody. I admit to a degree of professional pride. If you had seen Susannah six months ago you would understand what we have achieved."

"The royal we, Professor Higgins."

"I was not uniquely responsible for her recovery. But having witnessed it, neither did I feel that I could bear to see her go back to her old life; she would certainly have regressed rapidly and possibly, no, probably, become more disturbed than she was before. Hers was largely a depression caused by external factors."

"So you welcomed her with open arms into your life, into Aunt Judith's life, and encouraged her to wreck it."

Hector felt that Helen was being unfair. After all, he had also welcomed her into his life. He reflected that if George had not become ill during the night in Susannah's bedroom all this might well never have happened.

"We must hope that nothing has been wrecked. Judith is undoubtedly upset at the moment. But she and Susannah have developed a close bond. Possibly when she has become less upset and appreciates that her position is exactly the same as it has always been she will recover."

"But that's patently untrue. Aunt Judith was your wife, the person to whom you devoted yourself. Now she is just the little woman around the house and you intend to spend the rest of your days, or your nights, in the attic with Susannah. So her position is anything but exactly the same as it has always been. Anything but."

Helen's face was red. Her hair, usually untidy, seemed to have taken on an existence of its own, standing around her angry cheeks like a crowd of little boys cheering on the combatants in a fight.

Once again Hector felt that Helen was being hard on him. He had not indicated in any way that he intended to go on visiting Susannah in the attic. Obviously, at present that was out of the question.

His pipe had begun to glow and he puffed at it thoughtfully, conscious that his woes did appear to be resting a shade more lightly upon his spirits. Of course Judith would be all right. It was perfectly possible as the result of a shock to relapse into a temporary period of delusion without retreating permanently into this state. He turned his attention to Helen. She was over-reacting to the situation with great violence. It dawned upon him that Helen was not indulging in apologetics on behalf of Judith but on her own behalf. He decided that he would counter-attack.

"George's father," he said innocently, "will he help you with the baby when you return to Adelaide?"

"George's sodding father," Helen replied with an expression of frozen hatred on her face which now resembled the white, rugged slopes of a mountain inaccessible to humankind, "never helped anyone with anything in his life."

"Ah," replied Hector.

"The bastard told me that he was ready for marriage. Too true, he was ready for marriage. He'd been enjoying all the benefits of marriage in my flat for three years, treating me with a sneaky kind of solicitude which, busy as I was, I mistook for husbandly concern. When there were signs of the beginnings of George I assumed that he would stick around and adopt a fatherly attitude."

"You wanted . . . er . . . to settle down and get married and bring up a child in . . . er . . . a more or less conventional way," Hector suggested carefully.

"Did I buggery. I'm a career woman. But a woman isn't a woman until she's had a child," Helen exclaimed, thereby repeating her prevailing misconception about the nature of feminine purpose.

"Then you intended that George's father would adopt the role of the mother rather than the father," Hector said, "for obviously, whatever else it goes without, a baby must have a mother-figure and if you were going to continue to be a career woman you could not provide it with that as well."

Helen was getting flustered.

"I didn't intend anything. I just knew that I didn't want to get rid of it."

"And when he saw that he was cornered George's father took flight. Er . . . left," Hector added lamely.

"Pissed off and married a dolly bird," Helen concluded.

They sat in silence for some minutes, Hector now enjoying the comforts of his pipe which was going well, Helen contemplating with some gloom the prospect of returning to her demanding, rewarding, exciting job with George hanging around her neck like the albatross.

45

Susannah and Judith manoeuvred George into his sleeping suit as one might manoeuvre a duvet into its cover. He did not actually make the task impossible, but neither did he assist. His arms and legs, as with the corners of a duvet, never seemed to coincide with the arms and legs of his nightwear.

"We must let Murphy see him before we put him to bed," Judith murmured. "He always used to like to see the children last thing at night. It will cheer him up."

Hector had explained to Susannah.

"Well, it's really past his time," she said tactfully, "perhaps it would be better to let Murphy see him tomorrow night." Perhaps tomorrow night Murphy would have pissed off back to oblivion where he belonged. "Come on, you great fat boy. No, you're not going to eat the sponge. You've had your supper. It's up to the garret and off to sleep now."

Judith hung the towel over the rail and collected George's discarded garments to put them in the washing machine, folding each garment neatly. Then she followed Susannah up the attic stairs.

As Susannah placed the baby in his cot and tucked his bright cotton blanket around him Judith suddenly found herself besieged by a host of contradictory impressions. She sat down on the edge of Susannah's bed. Here Hector and Susannah had been happy. But Hector had been happy with her, too. Why had Hector come up here in the middle of the night, leaving her alone? He had come because he loved Susannah.

Judith gazed at the young woman, absorbed as she leaned over the cot, her brown hair falling forward in a smooth flood like the turfy waters of a brook, hiding her face. Judith did not, however, need to see Susannah's face. She knew well the expression it would be wearing. When Susannah was attending to George she thought about nothing else. It was not surprising that Hector loved her. She was mysterious in her affinity with the child, lovely with the endless enticement of the truly maternal.

The conflict arose because Judith was glad that Hector and Susannah had been happy, were happy together. In the same way that she had felt pleased when Murphy began to see more and more of his Susy, so she felt glad that Hector and Susannah were happy. But it was also the worst thing that had ever happened to her. Whereas with Murphy she had not ever been totally at one, she had invested everything in Hector, discarded all her props, thrown away her neuroses, left behind all the psychological structures up which her being had grown and to which it had clung as a virginia creeper clings to supports in a wall until it would be hard to say which was carrying which. Hector had been her contact with reality. Hector had put her in touch with herself. While she and Hector had been exclusively in love she had found out more about the nature of circumstances as they were understood by the young battling to assert themselves, the middle-aged battling to maintain themselves, and the old battling either to evade or eliminate their fear of dying, than she had known or understood before. She had been like an electrical current which can motivate all kinds of intricate and useful pieces of machinery when it is properly connected, but remains inert and void when it is not.

So what is to happen to me now?

"Murphy is jealous of Hector," she said miserably to Susannah. "He feels that I should never have deserted him. After all, we had been together for a long time. And now Hector doesn't really want me any more."

Susannah left the cot and sat down on the bed beside Judith.

She remembered the first time she had ever seen her, from the window of the ward, saying goodbye to Hector outside the flat as Judith was about to set off for work and Hector was coming in to the hospital. She had wondered how two middle-aged people could be so ridiculous about saying goodbye to each other for the day, what would make a silver-haired woman blush because she had been kissed by a large psychiatrist. She knew, now. She understood. She knew that Hector was Judith's link with the ordinary world of ordinary people, that without him she lived in a confused limbo of half-heard voices and misconceptions. She also knew that Hector had established himself, as it were, on the top of Judith's head, that he had recreated his unsatisfactory life on the foundation of Judith's devotion, that she had given him his first real home, and that he had taken all this and then become restless because it was not enough.

"You've been nicer to me than anyone," she said simply, putting her arm around Judith's thin shoulders. "You've taught me how to do things and I've stolen from you. Everybody takes everything from you, don't they? Nobody gives you anything back." She began to cry, very quietly, resting her head against Judith's head, clutching her awkward hands.

Judith was shocked.

"No, dear, you haven't taken anything from me. Of course you haven't. We've been very happy, the three of us. We've been very happy these last few months, doing the house, and then the baby and so on." She felt a great surge of love for Susannah.

Then she remembered, feeling her hands uneasy in Susannah's warm, new hands, and noticing their round, unbitten nails, that something had happened.

She had hated this girl. Why had she hated Susannah? When had she hated her? What could Susannah possibly have done to her, Susannah who was one of her children?

She couldn't remember.

"Now, don't cry, dear," she said, patting the young woman's arm, "don't cry any more. We'll all have a good night's rest. Maybe it will seem clearer in the morning.

Murphy can sleep on the sofa."

46

Helen had begun to think about her own problem. Without actually defining it Hector had pointed out to her that she had one.

She thought about the clatter of the office, the sound of typewriters and laughter, the half-cynical, half-saintly devotion to stories, the urgency and tension of interviews with their occasional dramatic surprises and their habitual, routine boredom. She thought about returning to her flat, now devoid of its male acolyte, the lonely realisation she always had that for her the office was real and other parts of her life were an elaborate fiction. Perhaps she, too, was a schizoid depressive. Perhaps she had inherited from her grandparents the same genes which made Aunt Judith strange. She realised only too well watching Susannah caring for George that for her having a baby had been an incident, something to joke and talk about at parties, while for other women it was a different ball-game.

She thought about the beach with its endless white-hot sand and vast blue-green waves; the tough, extrovert sportsmen and women speeding themselves over its bosom in boats, on surf-boards or on water-skis.

Thinking about it she realised without astonishment that she had never belonged there. It had not been her scene. As a child she had listened with fascination to her father's stories about England and longed for its intimacy, its dedication to detail.

She was glad that she had been. She was glad that she had given birth to George. What a story that would make, the revelation of her aunt's condition, the strange establishment she had gathered around her. But it was time for her to go home. She was eager to go home and begin it.

"Susannah," she said at breakfast, while Judith was outside saying goodbye to Hector, "Susannah, are you going to live with them, I mean, are you intending to stay for a long time?"

"How should I know?" Susannah shrugged.

"Well, I just thought . . ."

"I don't know. I don't know anything." Susannah had not slept well. She had lain awake listening to the sound of conversation from the room below, wondering what was going to happen next. She had lain awake remembering every word that Hector had ever spoken to her, especially each word that he had spoken to her in the attic, in her bed. She had wished that his voice which she could hear from the room below had been coming from the pillow beside her.

She supposed that she would have to go.

"Could you get a job?" asked Helen. "Do you like working?"

"I've never had a job so I don't know. It's not easy to get jobs, especially if you have no qualifications. But I can manage on Social Security, I don't have to starve. They don't let you starve, you know. Not quite."

"But isn't it awful, not having any money, not being able to lash out occasionally?"

"I don't want anything. Except cigarettes. If there's anything I want I don't have cigarettes until I've saved up. But I never want anything. Not for long. It wears off, you know, wanting things."

Helen tried to imagine not wanting things and failed. There was always something that she wanted. Not necessarily things, but prizes, goals, successes. If you didn't want something, what was there to keep you going? Georgie, for example. She had wanted Georgie. But Susannah was right. Whatever you wanted, it wore off. Whereas Susannah told herself beforehand that it would wear off, she always had to go on until she had achieved whatever it was and then make the discovery anew. Coming to England. She had wanted that. And it had worn off. She wanted to go back now, back to where she didn't belong. Georgie. Georgie had worn off. She had to go back to where she didn't belong with a baby which didn't belong to her. The prospect seemed uninviting.

"You wouldn't like to look after George for me, I suppose?" she said to Susannah. "I'm going to find him a bit of a drag."

"You bitch. You unutterable bitch. You're his MOTHER," Susannah screamed.

"Well, don't get upset about it. I only wondered." Were English people all so edgy? It had only been a casual proposition, a passing idea. "I know you're attached to him. I just thought you might like to keep him, you know, either come to Australia with me, or keep him here, adopt him or something."

Susannah threw to the floor a pile of plates that she had been carrying. She picked up a mug from the table which was half-filled with coffee and flung it at Helen. Helen ducked and the mug broke into fragments, splashing coffee which trickled like a map of an unknown continent down the recently painted kitchen wall.

As if he had already been tuned in, George, outside in his pram enjoying the yellow morning sunshine, hearing the sounds of destruction from within, began to howl.

Judith returned to find Helen on the floor with Susannah sitting astride her thunderstruck body flailing it with her small, clenched fists.

Judith sighed and went outside to comfort George.

Life was like that. One had these dreams. But they always turned out otherwise.

47

September had struggled over the moors like a farmer searching for a heifer that has strayed, encouraging the late raspberries in the crevices of the walls, urging on the blackberries, hastening the thistledown across the turf, thickening the coats of the shorn sheep, lowering the cloud hanging heavy and still like grapes in a silent, humid greenhouse.

Nothing had been decided. Nothing had been resolved. Nothing had happened. It was as if summer which had brought on the storm which threatened to topple Hector's delicately balanced edifice, was simmering on towards winter unexpressed except in subdued grumbles and occasional flashes of lightning only perceived after they had vanished.

"Well," said Tulip to Judith, "it is a grand place to live. I'm very glad I came. I did think, halfway up the hill, that what with the buses stopping so far away and me not being sure how to get here I might call it a day and go straight home but you know me. A bugger for being curious. I thought, I wonder where the hell this village is. If Judith used to be able to get to work every day I must be able to do the journey in reverse. Missed you, too. Wanted to look you up and find out how you liked being a lady of leisure. How do you like being a lady of leisure? It's a great life. I wouldn't mind being a lady of leisure. Country residence. Beautiful garden. Not having to get up in the morning." She paused for breath.

Judith filled her teacup.

"It's lovely to see you, Tulip. I've missed you as well." This was true. She had missed Tulip. She had missed her colour, her vivacity, her optimism. Also, the money that she would have been earning at the packaging firm would have come in useful. She could have saved it up against the day when Hector might decide that he wanted to marry Susannah. And Murphy's sandals were worn out. She could have bought him a new pair. Also, where was she going to live if Hector decided to marry Susannah. She couldn't stay if she were no longer needed. She did not believe in not pulling her weight. She had already been made redundant on several occasions in various ways. It was not a pleasant situation in which to find oneself, knowing that one had been superseded. As soon as Murphy and Hector had made up their minds what they wanted to do she would make a move. She would not wait until she became an embarrassment, something that everybody had to walk around in order to get to wherever they wanted to go. The money from the packaging firm would have come in handy. She had, of course, the money which was the proceeds of the sale of the house in Mackworth Street, but that was capital and you didn't spend capital. Aunt Phyllis had taught her that. If Aunt Phyllis had been of no practical use about anything, she did understand money.

Judith had missed Tulip. She had missed her badly. Tulip's problems were always an enjoyment and led one to believe that problems were for a laugh, not for keeping one sweating with terror during the long hours of the night.

"The girls should be back with the baby soon. They've taken him up the road in his pram. You'll like the baby. He's astonishing," she said.

"Babies are all alike. A load of trouble, babies. Can't see why people are gone on them," Tulip replied agreeably.

Tulip would have liked a baby more than anything. She took care not to get in the family way with the men for whom she amassed her treasurehouse of lacy underwear to enhance her treasurehouse of physical allurements. But she would be pleased when her sod of a husband finally got himself to England to give her a batch of proper babies with eyes like glowing embers and cheerful grins and glistening curls and skin the colour of smooth golden beech leaves. Though she supposed that if she had an English fella that she liked as much as she liked her sod of a husband she wouldn't much mind about the details of any babies they made between them. "But I expect I'll like George," she added generously. "After all, he's your nephew, and I like you."

"Great-nephew," Judith corrected. "Murphy's grandson."

"Who's Murphy?" asked Tulip.

"Oh, Murphy's my husband," said Judith.

"I thought Hector was your husband," said Tulip.

"Hector is and he isn't," said Judith.

"He is and he isn't?" asked Tulip.

"You see, he's in love with Susannah, but Murphy needs me. He got it out of his system."

"Murphy got what out of his system?" Tulip was becoming confused. After all, she had been born and bred in Lancashire. She thought she knew about Lancashire customs. Was this one that she had missed?

"Thinking that there is something else, something more important that the ordinary one doesn't supply but somebody else does."

"I see," said Tulip, who didn't see.

"We're back," shouted Helen from the front door.

"Oh good," said Judith. "We're out here in the kitchen. Tulip's come to visit us. Bring George for her to look at."

Susannah appeared with George in her arms. She was surprised to find the kitchen radiant with the diffused aura of Tulip, who was wearing a salmon pink sari with white silk trousers and her best gold earrings, a diamond gleaming like the morning star in the side of her nostril, her hair glowing like coal at the coalface, glistening in the first light to shine upon it since the emergence of man.

George crowed with amazement.

Tulip held out her arms and Susannah handed him over. George took one of Tulip's braids in his fat fists and shoved it into his mouth as a hungry monkey stuffs itself with a banana.

"He'll dribble all over you," Susannah warned.

"I've been dribbled on before," Tulip replied, bouncing

George who was trying to decide which was more enjoyable, the crunching of Tulip's hair or the feeling of being lurched around by her knees. He almost lost his composure in the curled up laughter which came over him.

Helen felt very proud. You had to say this for the English. They were not racist. After all, Tulip was obviously a Pakistani. It was nice to think that her son had taken to a Pakistani, at his age. She would like him to grow up conscious that the world was not divided by the colour of people's skins. Even though it was. She must take this opportunity to find out about the problems of immigrants living in Lancashire. She could write an article about it when she returned to Adelaide. She began her interview.

"Where do you come from?" she enquired in a kindly way.

"Who, me? Outskirts of Ostle." Tulip tickled George's ear with her other plait and he spread his round toes in an ecstasy of amusement, still chewing the first one.

Helen hesitated.

Perhaps Tulip came from some far-flung village so primitive that the date was calculated by the memory of the year in which the water buffalo with the white star on its forehead had fallen in the stream and broken its leg. Perhaps she had lost all her children in a terrible time of drought. Perhaps she was still trying to become accustomed to the Post Office and the Telephone and Money. Perhaps she had trailed through famine and disaster surrounded by her family to reach this land of plenty. She thought for a few moments before she qualified her previous question:

"No, before that I mean."

"Never been further than Manchester in me life," said Tulip cheerfully.

Susannah grinned.

Trust Helen to get hold of the wrong end of the stick. The part of Farringham in which Susannah had grown up was full of Pakistanis, Patans, Bangladeshis, most of them as Lancashire as she was. They were not all as gorgeous as Tulip, or as emancipated, but many of them, while clinging to their own customs, shared her good-natured toleration of their British hosts, many of whom were less tolerant than they were and with less reason.

"So you're Murphy's grandson," Tulip said conversationally to George, wiping a long tentacle of dribble off her chest.

George agreed with a windy smile. It was all one to him. He belonged to anybody who had something for him to put in his mouth.

Helen and Susannah fell into a thoughtful silence.

"Not the only one, of course," Judith added hastily. "Murphy has many grandchildren. He isn't interested in them until they are old enough to go on the stage. Treading the boards, you know. Likes children to develop along Thespian lines."

"I see," said Tulip, who didn't know what Thespian lines were.

But then, there's nowt so queer as folk.

48

When Helen took George back to Australia in October Susannah's engine ground to a halt, like an old steam-roller which has been kept going by loving ingenuity until its owner dies.

"Murphy does not exist," she screamed at Judith. "Once all. There is nothing in the world which has any reality. Bloody Murphy does not exist. Nothing exists. Nothing at all. There is nothing in the world which has any reality. Nothing. We're all just blobs of skin and bones waddling around the planet held on by gravity and kept on the move by our need to eat. There's fuck-all anywhere except our need to eat. And Murphy doesn't need you or anyone because what doesn't exist doesn't need to eat."

"Careful, Susannah." Hector felt a great sense of gratitude. He had thought about the problem until he could think about it no more. Explaining to Judith that although he was in love with Susannah he also loved and needed her had not worked. Murphy had established himself in the household tenaciously, like a dog of uncertain temper which must be skirted round warily because it is sure of its territory and feels the need to guard it constantly although it cannot distinguish between intruders and those to whom the territory truly belongs.

Now it had been savagely attacked, as it was wont to attack others. Even though Hector felt anguished by its suffering he knew that this had been unavoidable. Such a beast is not disposable in any other way.

Judith sat at the table alone after Hector and Susannah had completed the washing-up in silence.

She knew that Murphy did not exist. She had always known that Murphy did not exist.

But in his place she had put loving Hector, whom she had imagined to love her. Now she knew that this had been as much an illusion as Murphy was. If Hector had loved her, how could he have climbed the attic stairs and slept with Susannah, how could he have shared with Susannah the deep, fathomless wells of his comfort, the comfort which he had promised to her alone on their wedding day, surrounded by flowers, surrounded by glory, in the presence of good friends who were witnesses? How could he have left her alone when to take himself away from her and give himself to somebody else had caused her such paroxysms – like those a diver experiences when his oxygen supply is cut off and he moves swiftly towards death. Her brother, George, had died like this. Out in America, her brother George, diving for an oil company, had died on his way to the surface, left by a mistake without the correct amount of air. But George's death had been an accident. Hector had gone to Susannah's room surely knowing that she, Judith, would die.

She sat weeping, mute and desperate, conscious of nothing except Susannah and Hector, watching the news on the television set in the next room, torn between their love for each other and the strain that not expressing it again after that brief, guilty night had imposed upon them, and their concern for her, their impossible need to redeem the irredeemable.

Her thoughts began to settle down, to graze quietly in the knowledge that the three of them were still together, still trying to please one another, that Susannah was like a daughter to her, that Hector had not been able to help himself, that their household worked as well as most households and a lot better than many. Then some invisible hazard, some terrifying prospect which could not be identified, drove them into a little cluster of fear and sent them scudding away across the hillside, leaving her mind empty and desolate in a rain of jealous grief.

49

Late in October there was a letter for Susannah. It was the first letter she had received since she came to live with Hector and Judith.

The letter was from Helen. It contained a photograph of George, naked as the day he entered the bathroom of this life, even browner than he had been when he left England, being grasped by a pair of large, capable-looking hands whose owner had been left out of the picture. George was stretching his fat legs urgently towards a body of scintillating turquoise water. This water, the letter explained, constituted the swimming pool of Helen's Editor who had taken to George as had everyone else. The letter also offered detailed descriptions of George's progress, couched in a jaunty style, these details having been passed on to Helen by the young woman whom she had acquired to take care of him, having discovered, as she suspected, that there were plenty of Susannahs in Adelaide.

The letter was typewritten and faultlessly laid out. It communicated a deep feeling of affection and warmth which although it was an inherent part of her character she had not felt able to express adequately to the English while she was actually among them.

Susannah read the letter at the breakfast table and stared moodily at the sunny image of George while Judith read it aloud to Hector, exclaiming with admiration as she absorbed the wonders of the baby's development and laughed at his exploits and conquests as described by Helen.

Susannah felt a stony silence at the centre of her being, as if where her heart had beaten there was no longer a muscle, pumping around her body the forces which made her human rather than inorganic. She had a curious sense of foreboding, as if about to embark on an unknown journey over an alien sea on a huge vessel and she had neither locker nor berth. She watched Judith and Hector enjoying Helen's letter and knew that something momentous was going to happen to her.

Judith was no longer deluded. She had come to terms with Hector's peccadillo. Like many women, and, of course, many men, she had resolved to make the best of things and keep going. Under the happy exterior which attempted to make Susannah as welcome as she had always been, Judith was no longer living in a land of endless sunshine. Perhaps in this respect, too, she had taken another step towards recognising reality. But Judith's very acceptance of the situation, the fact that she went to sleep in Hector's arms every night prepared to wake and find him departed to Susannah's bed, had changed Susannah's perception of herself, and it had also changed her perception of Hector.

She now knew that Hector was not for her. He had given her himself. She had given him herself. But she knew that to take him from Judith would be unthinkable and that in any case he had not the slightest intention of abandoning his wife. Also, Susannah did not want him. He was too comfortable. Out of his torrents of comfort he had cured her. But she had repaid him for that by being cured. She no longer wanted comfort.

She had coped with the departure of George as she would now be able to cope with everything. She would save her rage for things that she could do something about.

She examined the feeling she had that she was embarking on a journey.

Handing the photograph to Judith she took back the letter and read it again, this time allowing herself an occasional smile.

George was hers. She was one of his godmothers. Wherever he grew up and however he grew up, part of him would always belong to her. She would see George again. She was sure of that. It was just a question of the time and the place.

She wondered whether she was about to die.

She decided to go and visit her mother.

50

Hector was making strange, gasping sounds as he slept.

Judith woke and lay beside him, horrified.

Was he having a heart attack?

She switched on the light and heaved him over on to his back so that she could look at him.

He opened his eyes. Without his glasses he could not see Judith. He was crying.

"Susannah," he said, "I'm sorry. I'm so sorry." Then he began to wake up fighting through the overheated mists of his dream as a tired man struggles across a waterless terrain. When he reached the edge of it Judith switched the light off again and held him in her arms.

Hector knew that this was Judith and he shook with sorrow.

"I've caused you a lot of pain," he said. "I've caused you both a lot of pain."

"Shh," said Judith. "She'll hear you."

"I've treated you very badly. I've treated you both very badly."

"It was only a dream," said Judith.

"No, it wasn't a dream. It was reality. It was the sort of reality that stupid, clumsy people like me blunder into and then regret."

"You couldn't help it. It was because you have so much love. Too much just for me. You had to love Susannah too."

"It was the worst possible thing I could do, for her, for you, for me, for all of us."

"No. No." Judith would have taken Hector upstairs herself and installed him in Susannah's bed if she had thought that it would make him happy, and if she had been sure that

Susannah would not be in a mood and order them out of her room. It occurred to her that even in her unhappiness she had felt a certain relief, a certain obscure delight in knowing that Susannah had made Hector happy. It vindicated some of her own shortcomings, compensated for her lack of youth and beauty, alleviated the sense of responsibility she felt in having Hector to please. "I don't mind. I don't mind at all. Nobody belongs exclusively to somebody else. We have to share each other. You need Susannah. And she needs you."

"Susannah doesn't need me any more. And I never needed her. I just wanted her, which is different. Quite different, Judith. You must understand that."

Exhausted by his dream and by his problems Hector drifted back to sleep, feeling the beginnings of his customary state of well-being, absent since the onset of indisposition in the conscience.

And Judith, holding his head against her breast as his breathing became regular and calm once more and her arms ached with the weight of his body, suffered the physical discomfort as a kind of punishment for having doubted that he loved her, remembering that she had forgiven Murphy's wickednesses and then remembering that Murphy didn't exist, that there was no Murphy. She knew that she was still travelling through the forest with Hector and that though some of its trees were now gleaming silver and stark, stricken by lightning, the forest was still enchanted.

51

Although it was in a different house the room was the same as it had always been. Entering it, Susannah felt the same sense of despair. Its dank ugliness struck her like an angry hand. She remembered how hard she had tried to brighten it up as a child by growing and nurturing geraniums. These terraced houses could be made beautiful with imagination and love. But her mother had never possessed either.

The presence of her mother's bed added another dimension to the room's atmosphere of hopelessness.

A young priest sat by the bedside, clutching a bunch of flowers. The sick woman turned her head wearily on the pillow and gazed at Susannah as if the effort of looking was drawing the last drops of strength from her body.

"You've taken long enough to come and visit me," she said by way of greeting her daughter. "Who told you I was ill?"

"Nobody. I just came."

Susannah was appalled. She had only been in the house for five minutes and already black, purposeless despair was descending upon her. As she had felt when she was a child, now again she felt helpless, confronted by a mother who was no mother, who would take nothing and had nothing to give.

She removed the flowers from the young man's hand and went away to search for something to put them in. All she could find was an empty milk bottle. She filled it with water and arranged the few roses as well as she could, pouring into this small task her old need to challenge the desolation of that miserable front room. Her knees were shaking.

"They smell nice," she said guardedly to the young man.

He gave her a wan smile. He had no idea who she was, and Susannah's mother made no attempt to tell him.

"How long have you been like this?" Susannah asked.

"I don't know." The invalid closed her eyes.

"Several weeks," the young priest replied.

"Who's been looking after you? Where's my stepfather?"

"Clifford's looked after me. He's a good son, my Clifford. He'll be home from school before long. He takes good care of me."

"Mr Briggs is . . . he's . . . er . . ." the young man began.

"Don't tell me. I can guess. He's in the nick." Susannah knew that she was lost. Her mother was terminally ill and had no one to look after her. Remembering Clifford she could imagine what kind of care he had been providing. It was now three years since she had left this house, with her own son, and gone to live a few streets away and never come back.

She wished that she had not come back now. If she had not come back she would not have known. She would not have been drawn once again into this sluggish current of hopelessness.

She looked at her mother's yellowish-white face with its tight skin and dark patches under the eyes. Her hair was grey and spread untidily over the pillow like a sprawl of vine leaves. The bedclothes were thin and stained. Her mother's hands, bony and twisted, pinched a fold of the discoloured blanket and twitched it again and again, as if by this movement she could somehow express all that was left of her will to live and keep herself going until Clifford came home from school.

Susannah felt a revulsion which made her want to run away from this squalor, back to Judith, back to her attic with its white and gold furniture, back to Hector. But she also felt a need to take this poor creature who was her mother and lay her in a clean bed in a warm, dry room and offer her once again the love which she had rejected when Susannah was a child.

She knew that whatever she did for her mother would provoke no response, generate no warmth between them. Her mother was past responding to kindness. She probably only looked forward to Clifford's arrival so that some need of his could galvanise her into another faint, anxious stir of what passed in this house for ordinary human feeling.

She knew, too, that her days with Hector and Judith were over. She could not leave her mother like this. She would have to come and care for her.

Her voyage had begun. She could see nothing but endless waste. No landmarks. No horizon.

The young parson was looking at her closely.

"The roses are from the vicarage garden," he said apologetically. "Nobody has done anything to it for years. They've gone completely wild. It seems a shame that they shouldn't be enjoyed. I don't have time," he added, wilting in the heat of Susannah's stare.

Susannah sensed his discomfort and despised him. He was about the same age as herself, she thought, dismissing him as a do-gooder and turning her attention to her mother.

"Have you had medical help?" she asked. "I mean, somebody must be looking after you. People aren't just allowed to rot."

"Father Harrison has been to see me several times since Father Wormold left us." Something in the wishy-washy waters of the soul of Janet Briggs recognised her daughter's dismissal of the visitor.

"Very kind of him, I'm sure. But what about a doctor?"

Susannah was desperate to ask where Father Wormold had gone. She remembered his visits during her childhood as among the few bright moments in an otherwise gloomy existence.

"Poor Father Wormold. He was a saint." The young parson appeared to have read her thoughts. "But he had a good end, God rest his soul."

God rest his soul.

Susannah had a sudden feeling of communion with Father Wormold. Yes, God would be resting his soul. God would be getting something out of Father Wormold. God would be enjoying him.

To her astonishment she began to cry.

She was not crying because she was going to be living in this dismal house again. She was not crying because her mother had not noticed that she had changed from the Susannah of the past to a new, vivid Susannah. It was not angry, choked crying. It was not the deep crying of unendurable grief.

She was crying because she was glad that Father Wormold's soul was being rested by God. She was crying because she would see George again. She was crying because she was going on a journey, and although she didn't know which port the ship was bound for, she knew that by bringing her back to the haunting face of her mother and the dirty smell of despair it was also going to free her from them forever.

52

"Perhaps I should go back to work now."

Judith was not exactly missing going to work. Tulip, having found her way to the house, had been finding her way back almost every Saturday, enchanted by the garden, by Hector, by the relaxed atmosphere so unlike the atmosphere at home where her ebullience was treated with a mixture of disapproval and resignation. Judith saw Tulip regularly. And Pat and Gill had been coming all summer whenever they could in an extremely old jalopy which Gill had acquired and which she drove with a kind of short-sighted enthusiasm which amounted to an endless saga of near-misses, like fishermen's stories. So she had also seen Pat and Gill. She had come to know her neighbours in the adjoining cottages, too, not well, but well enough to visit them and pass the time of day over a cup of tea when Hector was at the hospital. Susannah, of course, came to visit her every few days. Unable to bring herself to leave her attic completely she had simply taken a few clothes and possessions necessary to live the spartan life she was living at her mother's home. She came back to Hector and Judith's care as often as she could.

But the summer had long been over and Judith could not see that Tulip would want to trail half a mile from the bus stop in snow, or that Gill's monster would make it up the hill when the roads got bad.

"Uh-huh," Hector replied. "Three months as a housewife and you are tired of the job. I'd give you a very bad employment record."

"Oh, Hector, it isn't that." Judith always hopped straight into Hector's little traps. "It's just that, after all, I stopped work to be here to help with George and I feel unnecessary now that he has gone – though I enjoy being at home and there is always plenty to do."

"That's decided then," said Hector agreeably, "you're going to stay at home and do wifely things."

"Mind you, I wouldn't like to be like Phyllis and Iris. Not ever having to work was what made them so odd, I believe. And it's the same blood, Hector, it's the same blood. What about me? What about Murphy and all those other things? I could become like Phyllis and Iris, if I didn't have the routine."

"Judith, my dear. Nothing could persuade me that you would ever become like Phyllis and Iris. I mean, can you imagine being convinced that you were pregnant when you hadn't a shred of evidence?"

"Hector, that was different, as you know very well. When I thought I was pregnant I was making a perfectly logical deduction. We had made love. I had developed symptoms."

Judith tried to sound severe. She had been good at it when the children were small. She could make them quail even though she was shaking with laughter inside. But she could never manage it with Hector. Even now when she knew that she would always feel the sadness of understanding his need for someone else as well as herself, she still felt the laughter of complete trust rising up in her like an otter gliding to the surface of a river when she saw him observing her with an expression of concerned interest in his green-blue eyes as if the whole question had not been a joke.

"A very understandable deduction," he said. "But you forgot to follow it up with a pillow."

"Hector," Judith pointed out earnestly, "Hector, you are getting confused. It was Aunt Phyllis who had pillows to substantiate her phantom pregnancies."

After all, Hector was not one of those beautiful people who make many other people feel hungry but never feed anyone. Hector was an everyday person for whom every day was new, important, and led to the next day only in terms of its own satisfactions. This was why his passion for Susannah was so terrible and also why it had enlarged rather than diminished his relationship with Judith. This was why the storm while it raged had been so devastating for them: Hector was like an old man who can remember no past and see forward into no future so that the present when it was happy seemed glorious and when it was sad seemed intolerable.

Yet it had subsided into a calm, golden evening rich with colour and sweet with the aftermath of fury.

53

"You could have spared half an hour, just half a bloody hour, to do this," Susannah grumbled, ruthlessly hacking at the undergrowth in Josiah Harrison's garden. "You could have made this place nice and opened the gates to let some of them in to enjoy the roses growing. They die if you pick them, you know. They just bloody die."

Josiah Harrison eyed his helper with a mixture of curiosity and amusement. In the past few weeks when she had left her mother's bedside to escape its suffocating gloom he had become used to her extravagant outbursts and no longer felt cowed by her scorn.

"I've never come across a rose that didn't die anyway," he replied mildly, "and it seemed better to pick them and distribute them to the housebound than to let them die in situ since I hadn't time to put the garden in proper order. It's a good idea, though. If you'd like to take on the job we could open the gates next summer. There are some old benches in the cellar of the school that we could arrange in appropriate places for the elderly to sit on and enjoy the flowers."

"You'll have to plant a few flowers first. This lot's all bloody weeds. It's a miracle that anything has survived. The rhododendrons are all right, and some of the other shrubs. But look at this. Just look. Those are azaleas under there. I thought God's people were meant to take care of God's bloody creations?"

Josiah pushed the rusty mower up and down what had once been the neat vicarage lawn. He had found it in the derelict shed of the high-walled wilderness in the centre of the overcrowded human wilderness which was his parish.

Of course she was being sarcastic. Her remarks about

God's people and God's creatures were always intended to convey disbelief and disapproval. But this didn't matter to him. After all, nobody disbelieved or disapproved more than he did – comdemned to spend the rest of his life empty inside, tending the dying and trying to succour the living, ploughing his own wilderness because he had made a vow when the faith had been real and strong in him.

Susannah piled her garden prunings on a bed which she had cleared and shouted over the uproar of the mower, "We'll need to burn this. There's more dead than alive."

Yes. There was more dead than alive. It was just a question of going on. You knew that it was all an illusion. You knew that it had been a mistake. You knew that, as a member of the Revolutionary Communist Party in your university days, you had been nearer to the truth than you were to the Truth now. You knew that the madness which had driven you to train for the priesthood and become ordained had indeed been madness, a kind of thick spell like the spell of the honeymoon which sooner or later turns into piles of washing-up and dirty nappies and household bills – huge mountains of despair, in the presence of which you have to keep saying reassuringly, 'I love you.' Thank God, at least, that his honeymoon had been a solitary one, his love-affair, marriage and awakening to reality something deep and hidden, not reported in the local press for all to ponder. It was easier to pretend that you were still in love when nobody but yourself knew what was going on in your existential household.

"I'll get some petrol."

He couldn't find any petrol. The can which he kept for his old car was empty. But Father Wormold had warmed the upstairs landing of the chilly building with a paraffin heater and he managed to extract a jam jar full from the base of this.

"Paraffin. Stand back in case it flares."

He emptied the jam jar over the mound of branches, leaves and withered plants and flung a lighted match into the heart of it.

The light was beginning to go. It was not dark, not even twilight, just the faint time between afternoon and evening when everything shivers in anticipation of the night to come.

The fire erupted like a volcano. With a cry Susannah leaped away from it and stared into its ferocious beginnings from the edge of the erratically mown grass.

Joe looked at her, surprised. Apart from her tears when she had realised that Father Wormold was dead it was her first expression of spontaneous feeling in his presence. The rest, her social indignation, her bad temper, had been, he knew, like his preaching and parish duties, something that had to be done in order to keep going.

He wondered vaguely about Susannah. He had gathered something of her past from visiting her mother who without mentioning her daughter at all had managed to portray her various experiences as if they had been a personal affront against her.

She was what the Americans would call a tough cookie. Well, so was he. They had both been toughened in the world. He knew what it was, not to let go, not to let on. To go through the motions; smile, comfort and cheer, or in Susannah's case, rail and rant.

They stood and watched the fire. Large branches in its core glowed and shimmered, a crimson and scarlet substance, a divine other essence, something apart from what had created it. Flames crashed upwards through the twigs in zigzag, spitting utterances; sparks, vivid and potentially the start of conflagrations filled the garden like a sky full of vagrant stars. The damp leaves hissed and sighed, smouldering and steaming and pouring clouds of thick smoke which smelled of promise and renewal into the subdued half-light.

In spite of themselves the two tough cookies exchanged pleased glances.

A chorus of children's voices floated over the high wall from the street.

"It ain't Plot Night 'til next week. Wotcha burning for? We could've 'ad it."

"That's true," Joe said ruefully to Susannah. "Next year we'll save it until November the Fifth and beat them at their own game."

54

It was all neither one thing nor the other. Susannah was spending more and more time with Josiah Harrison and less time with them. Joe could always find a job for her to do.

Judith was learning to live with her new realizations and Hector was waiting. He did not know what he was waiting for. But there was something.

"Come and have supper with us, Alan," he suggested to his young registrar one day as they were drinking their morning coffee.

Why he suggested this he could not imagine. He simply said it. And as soon as he had said it he knew that it had been a good idea. During the time he had lived in Farringham Alan had disposed of, or been disposed of by three landladies. Hector had not delved into Alan's background and had no idea why landladies should present such a problem to him, and he could only guess at the reasons landladies might have for finding Alan a problem. He did not know why he had never thought of offering him hospitality before, perhaps while they still lived at the hospital. Somehow he and Judith had never felt the need to invite other people to their flat. Here in the cottage, now, it seemed the obvious thing to do.

They did not foresee, however, that he would turn up with a one-eyed cat.

"G..G..Garlic," he announced with a smile at the front door. "The c..c..cat's name is G..Garlic."

"Oh, isn't he lovely?" said Judith.

Hector was not so sure. One's visitors sometimes turned up carrying a bottle of wine, or they sometimes turned up carrying a box of chocolates, or a bunch of flowers. He didn't think he could ever remember hearing about a visitor who had turned up carrying a tom cat with half a tail, not much of either ear, and only one eye.

"G..G..Got him from F..Fred at the g..gate. Been hanging about. Asked me if I knew anyone who would g..g..give him a h..home. Probably comes from one of the m..m..mills. Been chewed, in p..places, by a r..rat."

Like the clouds parting to let the sun into the summer, Judith's heart opened to provide a refuge for this feline wreck.

"Poor thing," she crooned. "Of course we'll have him. Come on, old fellow. Let's find some milk."

"Not m..milk," Alan warned. "F..F..Fred says m..milk wreaks havoc with his insides. And n..nothing out of a t..t..tin. Fresh f..f..fish. And he likes g..g..garlic on it. Hence his name."

It occurred to Hector that youth and beauty are not the only, or even the most lovable qualities in the world.

He took Alan's coat and a very long scarf which had been wound three times round his head and twice round his throat. As he hung them up he watched Garlic drape his fat, ragged shape over Judith's shoulder. By the expression in his one grey eye and the tone of his baritone purr Garlic conveyed a sense of pleasure only to be found in those who possess true discrimination.

He knew when he had arrived in the right place at the right moment.

Though it was not exactly what he had been waiting for, Hector felt that this arrival was significant.

55

"I don't care how many bloody table tennis rackets you've wrecked before, you're not going to wreck any more. Why do you think all this has been set up? Why do you think the Church has provided you with a perfectly good hall in which to use some of your abundant spare time? So that you can practise your infernal destructive arts on your own amenities? So that you can extend your moronic empire? You bloody well get on and use the facilities properly. Norman is a good pianist. He enjoys playing the piano and the others enjoy listening to him. Every time you smash up the fucking piano you are interfering with the rights of the majority. So either push off and don't come back or settle down and do something constructive like the rest of us. And pick up those bits and put them in the bin. If I ever see you, any of you, smashing anything again, so help me I'll screw your balls off. This is a church recreation room. Not a nazi training squad."

Susannah stared at them, her eyes as wide as the eyes of an enraged bull.

The four youths stared at her, their shaven heads, studded belts and tight, tattered black clothing out of place amongst the other, tidy adolescents. She wasn't very big. They could certainly have done her, between them. But she had the edgy ferocity of a cat that has lived on the outskirts of a farm for the whole of its life and knows how to kill. They had no doubt she would fulfil her promise; one had to be careful.

"Think you're something, don't you?" muttered Fred with the white make-up and black lipstick. "Think you've got it all sussed, knocking off our parson. We belonged to this club since before you ever came down here. It's our club, to do what we like with."

"That it is not. Just because you've managed to bully and torment the rest of them for so long doesn't mean that you have exclusive rights. If you can't understand the difference between making things and knocking hell out of them I suggest you get yourselves off up to the corporation tip and practise on the rubbish."

Norman and Karen and Stephen and Kay and Cathy and Jamie and Agnes felt the crowns of their heads pricking with fear, as though they too had shaven heads. In the corner a little group of chess players, interrupted every week for the past many months and re-grouping once they had assembled their pieces and re-set the board, became aware through the swirling mists of their concentration that the uproar was not of the usual variety and turned to observe the unlikely scene. A couple of young lovers, dancing quietly to the subdued tones of the record player, stood still in each other's arms trying to disengage themselves from their mutual absorption to join forces with the others. The table tennis players, rolling up the net, also took an interest in what was happening. Nobody felt able to rush to Susannah's side or actively show their approval but a general sense of relief and well-being filled the old building, as though somebody outside had started to cook onions and they were all hungry.

Clifford, looking at his half-sister with astonishment, turned his attention swiftly back to the plant pot he was covering with shells at her instruction, for their mother. He supposed, resignedly, that Fred and Bruce and Smiffy and Warto would get him on the way home. They'd got him before. They'd get him again. She'd find out. They'd had helpers here before who'd tried to sort things out. It always ended the same way. They left. None of them had ever stood up to them like that though. He looked furtively at Josiah Harrison, who had just appeared in the doorway.

"I see our favourite members are here again," he said, approaching Susannah and realising with a sudden lift of his weary spirits that she was in a fit of murderous rage. "What have they achieved tonight?"

"The sodding little bastards have broken the piano again

and smashed all the table tennis bats. They should have been put down at birth," Susannah hissed.

"Come on. Let's go. This is getting boring," said Warto.

"Load of wet shithouses making a mess with paint like little babbies at nursery school," added Bruce.

"Let's go and start a riot outside the chippy," suggested Fred, brightening up.

"Just a MINUTE," roared Susannah. "Not one step towards that door. Not one step. You don't leave here until you have picked up all those pieces and put them in the bin."

Joe Harrison felt a flame of laughter leaping around in his gut, catching everything in sight and flinging it on to the bonfire which was beginning to engulf his personality.

She was so small. They were so big. But she made them feel something like fear.

The four heroes looked incredulously at Susannah.

"Do it yourself," said Smiffy, but he said it under his breath.

56

At the end of November Susannah finally left Hector and Judith's household. But she did not move her possessions into her mother's home. She moved into Josiah Harrison's vicarage as his housekeeper. Hector was depressed. He was not depressed in a serious, ill way. He was depressed in the way that a painter is depressed when he finishes a picture.

Judith, too, missed her bright, fierce, unpredictable visits. She felt, not relief that the cause of so much suffering had gone but a kind of new suffering caused by its absence. She felt now, as she had before, that she would suffer anything herself in order that Hector should be happy. This feeling persisted, in spite of the relaxation which stretched over the cottage like an elastic bandage taking the ache out of strained muscles. She found herself half hoping that Hector would take to and adopt another of his women patients.

This, however, was never going to happen again.

Hector, having envisaged the possibility of sharing a lifetime with Murphy, was so grateful to him for departing, and with relatively little fuss, that he settled down to enjoy, one day at a time, his work, his new home, his garden and his wife, who now seemed doubly dear to him, sure as he was that no matter what he did she would not cease to love him. Since he had come out of the cupboard into which he had put himself after the ending of his first marriage, he had always been uneasily conscious that, although this one was totally different, it too contained elements of instability, not all of them connected with Judith's indisposition.

He watched with contentment, as she fetched and carried, responding to his and the lordly Garlic's every whim. It was not that he simply liked being waited on, as some men do. It was not that he was too idle to do things himself, or incapable. He had managed to look after himself, after a fashion, for long enough. It was more an understanding between them that he would devote his energies to curing the world and she would devote herself to tending the sickness in him engendered during his privileged but lonely childhood.

At the hospital he was dynamic. At the hospital his active mind was engaged in challenges and rewards. At home, where he was no longer looking to Judith for an excitement which she could not provide, no longer preoccupied with the notion that somebody else might be more stimulating, a better foil for his wit, a sturdier companion during his mental journeys, a more powerful motive for his sexuality, he slid into a truly autumnal state, accepting the crimson and gold hues which his happiness wore as the trees wear their consummate leaves.

Once more he was king.

"Judith, my dear," he said as winter approached, seasonally, that is, not metaphorically. "How would you feel about letting young Judson have Susannah's room until he has found himself a house? It shouldn't be for too long. And you like him."

"Oh, Hector, what a good idea. It's a shame to waste that nice room. I'll buy some furniture for it and we'll make him some bookshelves. He can be quite comfortable up there, as Susannah was."

Susannah's white and gold trappings had gone with her to the dilapidated vicarage. Judith had insisted that she should take them and after protesting Susannah had gladly accepted, aware that they represented a kind of dignity to which she had aspired and which she had reached, if only by her fingernails.

"I thought you might think so. I haven't mentioned it to him yet, of course, but I shall do so tomorrow, and I'm sure he'll be delighted. He doesn't seem to be able to settle anywhere and the digs he has at present are getting him down."

Alan would take the place of Susannah, Helen and George.

Alan would provide Judith with little flurries of anxiety and satisfaction, his precarious welfare would become an additional source of activity for her fostering spirit.

Hector breathed deeply, forgetting that he had his pipe in his mouth. The thin blue smoke furrowed into his lungs. He coughed and choked for several minutes, thinking as he did so, that Alan would not present a threat to anyone.

57

Susannah wondered why she was doing it, going from street to street knocking on doors, talking to people she didn't know, following up vague pieces of information from uninterested neighbours in an attempt to trace her father. She didn't know why she felt that she had to tell him about her mother's death. But as she trailed up and down the desolate area she was haunted by her vision of the emaciated face, the mouth wide open after it had drawn its last breath, the grey hair tangled and pitiful in spite of her weeks of washing it and trying to make it pretty. She didn't know why she felt she had to tell her father about Clifford, standing by their mother's body overwhelmed by the grief which comes from seeing the nearest thing to human comfort in your life disappearing over the horizon like a small, dark shape which you are sure was a ship. After all, Clifford was nothing to her father. And she was nothing to him, either. She was also certain that, even if he remembered his wife after all these years, he would not be in the least bit moved to hear that she had died.

"Susannah," her mother had complained, "there is so much noise. Close the window. Nobody cares how I feel. It doesn't matter to anybody that I am so ill."

And Susannah had closed the window, thinking that in this way her mother had finally cut herself off, as Hector had cut the cord which bound George to his mother, with a quick snip of the scissors. But for George it had been the beginning. For her mother it was the end.

When her daughter had moved in to look after her, Janet Briggs had deteriorated rapidly, almost as if by becoming worse she could punish Susannah for not being there before. She ate almost nothing and the doctor, appalled at her state, began to visit her every day, partly to give her what help he could, partly to encourage Susannah, who was trying to cope with the difficulties as Judith would have coped with them.

She had begun by making Janet get up, bathing her, dressing her and settling her as comfortably as possible in the only armchair in the house, which though ancient and worn was still better than Janet's threadbare bed. Susannah would sit beside her on the floor, reading to her to pass the hours, looking in vain for some reaction from her mother. She performed one little task after another – making drinks and bringing them to her in a child's plastic beaker which she could hold more easily with her weak, misshapen fingers, cooking minute quantities of food and arranging them as if she had been preparing a doll's tea party. But she was conscious that her mother resented these efforts. It was as if by trying to improve her lot Susannah had made it doubly hard for her to bear. Even Janet Briggs knew she should feel grateful, and say so.

But this was of no consequence to Susannah.

She began to know every pain in the emaciated body, to anticipate every complaint, to provide every comfort that she could provide. And although there was no response, she knew that her efforts were another little protest about the unspeakable front room, like the one she had made when she grew the geraniums there as a child. Surely, in spite of everything, her mother's death was better than it might have been.

Now Susannah was driven on, from one clue to another, until she reached a council house on a respectable estate in one of the less poor parts of Farringham. She had been surprised when an elderly man, whose name she had been given by the sister of somebody who remembered him as a drinking companion, gave her this address, telling her that her father had moved there some years ago after which he had lost track of him as he had long stopped coming to their usual pub. Susannah, ever since she had become tormented by her desire to find him, had expected to find him as she remembered him, drunk and without hope.

She knocked on the nicely painted front door of the semi-detached, red-brick house with a gleaming bow window and the winter remains of a well-cared for garden. It was opened by a neat, round housewife of about Judith's age with black hair in which only a little grey shone, and eyes as young and optimistic as Susannah's mother's had been old and dull.

"I'm Susannah Redfearn. I'm looking for my father," Susannah said, coming straight to the point. "I was told to try here by somebody who used to know him."

The woman looked at her for a moment in silence. Then, to Susannah's astonishment, she drew her across the threshold and embraced her.

"Of course you are, love," she exclaimed, releasing her and examining her face at arm's length before giving her another hug with a smile which did not just involve her mouth or even her eyes but seemed to emanate from the whole of her person, like the faint, pleasant perfume which Susannah, close to the woman's body, felt enveloping her.

"Now, you come right in. I'll put the kettle on. Jim," she called over her shoulder, "Jim, come and see who's here. It's your daughter Susannah." Still calling in an excited voice she led Susannah by the hand to the door of the living room. She opened it, gently pushed Susannah inside and closed it behind her. Then she hurried away to the kitchen, leaving Susannah to find her father.

Jim Redfearn was standing by the fireplace, a pair of spectacles in one hand, a newspaper in the other, an expression of numb disbelief on his face.

They stared at each other. Instead of a thin, white-faced, angry child he saw a young woman wearing a red coat and a multi-coloured beret which she had knitted herself. This was perched at a jaunty angle on her handsome head. Instead of a huge, red-faced drunk she saw a middle-aged man of medium build with eyes which told her the story of his life in the ten seconds which elapsed before either of them spoke.

"I'm glad to see you, Susannah," he said at last.

"Well, Dad."

They stood looking at each other. Susannah couldn't speak. As when she had first begun to talk to Hector she had felt as if she were being suffocated, so now she struggled with the fear that if she didn't concentrate all her effort upon breathing slowly and deliberately she would asphyxiate.

Jim Redfearn wiped his eyes on his sleeve and then she was in his arms, a small, crying girl being comforted as was right and proper by her own, true father.

"She's dead, Dad. She died last week."

"I tried, Susannah. I did try. For a long time I tried."

He looked down at her, fishing in his pocket for a handkerchief, wiping her eyes, wiping his own eyes, rocking her in front of the fire, extinguishing with the evidence of his new life the years of anguish which were all that his daughter's childhood had known.

58

"A..m..mazing meal, Judith," said Alan Judson gratefully after the first supper he had eaten at the cottage as an inhabitant. "Mrs S..S..S..Schofield, my landl..l..l..ady kept t..t..trying to p..p..poison me. I think she was a des..des..descendant of the B..B..Borgia family."

"I'm glad you enjoyed it," Judith replied. She wasn't ever sure whether she should provide the word which was proving difficult or allow the young psychiatrist to continue until he had mastered it, but she supposed that he would improve as he came to know them better, and that she would find out as time went on whether he preferred to be helped or liked to struggle until it emerged. She decided for the present that she would allow him to finish his sentences.

"Have a drop more wine." Hector had noticed that Alan always arrived in the department looking very well – at least, with a good, fresh colour in his cheeks, which sometimes seemed to have spilled into his eyes, giving them a slightly glazed, over-used appearance. But it was not until now, when he had disposed of four glasses of sherry, three large gins and a bottle and a half of wine without being in the least bit affected by it, that he realised the young man drank like a dry lawn. Probably never got drunk. Just drank and drank. Understandable, really. Must have problems, impediment like that.

However, Hector found that trying to keep pace with Alan's drinking during the meal had somewhat blurred the edges of his perception. And he felt vaguely uneasy, as if somewhere the distant future began to take on an alien, troubled mien, altered by the prospect of providing or monitoring the consumption of rivers of alcohol.

"Y..Y..Y..Yes. Either that or she was a w..w..w..witch," Alan continued, proffering his glass and holding it steadily until the last of the bottle's contents was safely installed in it. "I th..th..th..think she got up at d..d..d..dawn and filled a sack with t..t..t..toads and other r..r..reptiles with which she made n..n..nourishing unsavouries."

"Oh, poor you," Judith exclaimed, partly referring to his landlady's cooking and partly to his speech. She could see that it was going to be a real challenge, making this very agreeable person feel happier so that he wouldn't be troubled like this in conversation.

Hector decided that for tonight, as it was Alan's first night in the cottage, and to help him adjust to the eccentric furniture with which Judith had recreated Susannah's room for him, he would let the booze flow without regard to cost or consequences.

It proved to be an evening which they were all to remember.

By the time they retired to bed at half past eleven even Alan was slightly the worse for wear.

"Well, how do you think you are going to like having a new lame duck?" Hector asked as he attempted to put both his legs into the same side of his pyjama trousers.

"Oh, I think he's l..l..l..lovely," Judith replied, throwing caution and good taste to the winds after having drunk two more glasses of wine than she normally drank.

As they climbed into bed they heard a sudden crash from the attic. It was repeated and before they could collect themselves it began to repeat itself at rhythmic, insistent intervals and the ceiling of their bedroom which was not under-drawn and therefore also constituted the floor of the room above began to rise and fall like the swell behind a motor boat, increasing in vigour and velocity until they had reached the landing outside Alan's door.

"Hello, hello?" Hector called, at the top of the attic stairs. "Hello, Alan? Are you all right?"

"C..C..C..Come in, do, do, do c..c..c..come in," Alan called back expansively, in a breathless voice.

Hector and Judith entered Susannah's bedroom.

Alan was bouncing up and down on the bed, holding the two end corners of the duvet in his hands.

"Er...what is the trouble?" Hector asked.

"N..N..N..No trouble. Just sh..sh..sh..aking the f..f..f.." Alan abandoned the word feathers and progressed to, "contents of this d..d..d..duvet to the b..b..b..bottom. Too hot all at the t..t..top."

As he bounced and the feathers bulged slowly towards the base of his bedcovering the young man rose higher and higher until he was just below the ridge pole of the attic roof.

"Oh dear," said Judith. "Do be careful."

"Look, old man," Hector began to explain, "the floor, it's the ceiling of our bedroom. Old house, you know. Very old wood. Quite a lot of give in it, but you, and the bed, you know what I mean. It's lurching about." Hector was beginning to regret the last two brandies, which had seemed fun at the time, but now appeared to be mocking his attempts to express himself clearly.

As he finished the word 'about' there was a sickening thud as Alan's head struck against the ridge pole of the attic roof. The young man dropped like a puppet whose strings have been loosened, and folded up on the duvet which was now nicely regulated according to his requirements. There he lay looking like a seraph under his halo of curls, an expression of peace and joy on his face.

"Nasty bump," said Hector, feeling the lump which was rising visibly on the top of Alan's skull. "He's out for the count."

"Oh dear," said Judith. "Oh dear. Oh dear. I could see it coming but there wasn't time to warn him."

"Now then." Hector tried to summon his professional supplies of calm-for-all emergencies. "Come on, old chap, you're all right," he suggested encouragingly to the unconscious form, patting its smiling cheek.

"What do we do now?" In a distant kind of way Judith knew she should be worrying, but the presence of Hector, with whom nothing really terrible was possible, and the warm comfort of unaccustomed alcohol in her stomach, gave her a distinctly unconcerned feeling.

"Better think of something," Hector murmured, more to himself than to his wife. He was trying to assess the perils of the situation. But as he listed Alan's possible injuries and offset against them the factors which indicated that he was probably all right, the two lists became confused and he couldn't remember which were danger signals and which were reassuring signs.

"Look, I'll tell you what," he said to his wife. "You go downstairs and telephone for an ambulance. But tell them not to hurry. By the time they arrive he may have come round. But perhaps he should be X-rayed in any case. Can't be too careful with heads."

Judith hurried down the attic staircase. She remembered that her father, Cecil, had been rendered unconscious by the weight that had dropped on his head on stage. Alan's head had been much more forcibly struck than that. She'd better not tell them not to hurry.

"Don't run," Hector called after her, taking Alan's pulse and struggling with calculations which allowed for alcohol and subtracted shock and added for possible haemorrhage all without the aid of his watch. "We don't want you with a broken leg."

Ten minutes later the ambulance arrived and she let the two men in at the front door.

"I'm awfully sorry you've been called out so late," she apologised as they clambered up the attic staircase in front of her, carrying a folded up stretcher.

"Not to worry, lady," one of them replied good-naturedly. "All part of life's rich pattern. Interrupted the strip-poker, that's all. Not much excitement tonight."

"But we'll have a problem with these stairs and the stretcher," the other one added.

The stairs to the attic consisted of a Slingsby ladder which had remained a fixture since Cecil, tired of the boys' habit of pulling it up behind them so that they could not be reached, had nailed it firmly at every possible point with six-inch nails so that it became an immovable staircase though it was, in fact, only a glorified ladder.

Entering the bedroom the two ambulancemen hesitated, possibly detecting on the air some of the evidence of the sherry, gin, wine, brandy and whisky which had found their way into the object of their rescue operation.

"Ah, here you are," said Hector nervously.

"Hello. It's Dr Jones, isn't it? Thought I recognised you. Live here now, do you? Used to live at the hospital, didn't you?" he asked, not waiting for an answer to his first three questions.

"Unconscious," he declared, examining Alan's happy form.

"Yes," replied Hector, as though this observation made everything a great deal clearer.

"He's drunk," the ambulanceman continued.

Judith stood patiently waiting for the experts to reach a diagnosis.

"I know he's drunk," said Hector, beginning to feel the least bit irritated. "But he's also had a nasty blow on the head."

"Had to subdue him, did you?" said the first ambulanceman with a wink. "Had a bit too much and got out of hand? With the wife, maybe?" He looked sympathetically at Judith.

"No, no, no, no, no," exclaimed Hector. "There was nothing like that. He was bouncing."

"Bouncing?" queried the second ambulanceman from the shadow of a titanic mahogany wardrobe which Judith had thought a suitable improvement for Alan's room. "Bouncing?"

"He was trying to get the feathers to the other end," Judith explained thinking how hard it was to make simple things obvious.

"I see. He was bouncing to get the feathers right." The first ambulanceman prepared to shift the body.

"Hit his head on the roof, you see," Hector concluded lamely. It did all sound rather implausible.

"Worse things happen at sea. Come on, Pat, let's get him down the road."

"Yes, I think he should be X-rayed. Just to be on the safe side."

Hector helped the two men to roll Alan on to the stretcher.

Judith held the door open as they tried to carry the victim to the top of the ladder.

"Now then, Pat, what do you think?"

"Never in a hundred years, Harry."

"He'll fall off." Hector summarised their dilemma.

After some deliberation they removed the uncomplaining patient from the stretcher, dangled him one step at a time down on to the landing below, then replaced him and transported him with dignity to the hospital where he was admitted to the casualty ward. There, a radiologist who was woken to X-ray his head, and everyone who examined him, from the casualty officer on duty to the nurses, to the radiographer himself pronounced Alan to be drunk and Hector, finding it increasingly difficult to keep his eyes open, agreed and went on to explain that he had also been bouncing and had suffered a head injury.

The following morning Alan was released from the casualty department and went straight to work in the wards, wearing a healthy, rubicund expression and unable to explain to either the patients or his colleagues why he had a large dressing on the crown of his head.

"There must be something about that attic," Hector thought, making the sort of decision that people make the following morning, that Alan's first night at the cottage must not be allowed to set a precedent.

59

"Now come on, lad," said Jim Redfearn to a white-faced Clifford, "shape yourself or we'll be late." But he said it in a kindly voice.

Clifford was sitting on the bottom stair trying to tie the laces of the new shoes which Betty had bought for him.

Jim looked at him with embarrassment.

Surely somebody's taught him to tie a bow. A boy of fourteen.

He sat down beside Clifford and began to pull the laces together in the first shoe, demonstrating.

Betty, wearing a beige suit with a red chiffon blouse which glowed under her chin and added to the rosy warmth of her general appearance, pretended not to notice what was happening, patting her hair and making a face at herself in the hall mirror, unnecessarily checking to ensure that her brooch was properly fastened. But her heart ached for Clifford, dressed in his new clothes and looking as lost as he always looked.

Clifford watched Jim's big hands deftly making the laces even, passing the right lace over and under the left lace, pulling the knot tight, forming a loop and passing the right lace around it, underneath to make the second loop, then pulling the two loops tight.

"There," said Jim, "that's not bad, if I say so."

Clifford's eyes filled with tears.

"There we are then. You do this one."

The thin fingers with their bitten nails copied Jim's movements with anxious care and when the laces were tied Betty exclaimed with delight.

"Good lad. It's not so easy when you've always worn

things without laces." It seemed an acceptable explanation.

Jim smiled at Clifford, a pleased, encouraging smile.

"Now then," he said. "Now then. That's grand."

And as he shepherded his wife and his new son out towards the old car which he kept going with skill and patience he wondered vaguely what Hector would make of them, and why he and that Judith had invited them.

I suppose he wanted to take a look at me. Susannah seemed to want to show me off. Seems she's talked to him about me. God knows what she found to say. Better to put all that behind us. Must be kindly people. Been good to our Susannah.

We're a droll crowd, though, to be going out for tea.

60

"Well, how should I know? He probably just wants to see us all together. It could be some kind of experiment. A follow-up." Susannah was trying to get the multi-coloured beret on at the right angle. It had to be right or the effect was lost.

"You're not a patient now, though. You're a friend." Joe Harrison fitted his plastic dog-collar into the slot at the front of his shirt collar and put his jacket on.

"But he's still a shrink. You know what shrinks are."

As she spoke these words Susannah felt a wave of guilt rising up and falling into the pool of her consciousness. This was Hector that she was talking about. How quickly we forget what's what.

61

"Look here, old man," said Hector, "you're going to find this a very interesting evening. But it's strictly for observing behaviour. Seeing how patterns are kept going from one generation to the next. And to get to know my pride and joy, Susannah. So we'll keep fairly well off the bottle."

"G..Gotcha. Clinical homework. Mixing b..business and pleasure, but tempering the social an..anaesthetic." Alan's speech had improved. After all, there was very little to make one feel inhibited in his new home.

"Well, I'm not observing behaviour," said Judith firmly. "I'm going to enjoy myself. Dear Susannah, and her father, and his new wife, and Susannah's parson friend, and poor Clifford; it's going to be a lovely evening with the house full of people as it used to be."

Hector watched his wife putting plates into the oven, arranging the flowers on the table for the twentieth time, placing the chairs where they would be best situated to allow conversation, looking for table napkins, stirring the soup. He thought, as he had thought a thousand times, that his wife, his beloved wife Judith, was a romantic. And then he remembered.

If you are a depressive you have got to search for and find ways of making life tolerable. And if you are a schizoid depressive you do that by finding possible, but sometimes unlikely, answers to its problems.

Then you are accused of being a romantic.

62

Garlic opened his one eye and surveyed the company. He was occupying the chair nearest to the fire and his mottled coat appeared to be shivering like a flame in its glowing. He watched the visitors coming in one by one, then, as was his wont, he chose the most likely human and made himself comfortable. The human he chose was Clifford.

Clifford was living in a vacuum left by the death of his mother. Having assumed that all women were like her, he found it difficult to adjust to Betty whose loving kindness he found incomprehensible. Susannah, of course, had been behaving towards him in a sisterly manner. But her concern was tempered by the feelings of resentment and disapproval she had entertained towards him since he was born. So he had not been well prepared for his new life.

He sat down in the corner at the other side of the fireplace and Garlic, who had idly monitored his progress from the front door through the welcoming ceremony in which everybody was talking about the state of the weather, flopped off his own chair and climbed clumsily on to the boy's knee. Clifford, nervously eyeing Hector and Judith and Alan, whose h..h..hello had frightened him considerably, began to stroke the cat's thick fur. The tension gradually left him as he realised that although he was the only child present he was not going to be made the focus of attention or humiliated by these adults. Garlic crawled up Clifford's chest being careful not to expose his careworn claws and draped himself over his thin shoulder like a moth-eaten stole. Clifford rested his weight on the corner of the low bookcase so that the cat would be firmly supported. He could feel the heavy warmth of its body. Garlic shifted his position and buried the square shape of his soft jowl in the hollow of Clifford's neck.

Clifford had never possessed a cat, or indeed any animal, and the casual trust which Garlic had bestowed upon him moved him deeply. He continued to stroke Garlic and Garlic turned up the volume of his purring so that Hector, who had been observing Clifford without appearing to take any notice of him, leaned across Susannah and whispered in his ear,

"You know that it is a great honour to be Garlic's friend. He doesn't take to everyone. He usually only associates with people who are likely to feed him."

"Would he like some food?" Clifford was anxious now in case he was not fulfilling his role as Garlic's chosen friend.

"Later. I expect Judith has something lined up for him. You can feed him later. Then he'll be your slave."

"How did he lose his eye?" asked Clifford who was beginning to forget how nervous he felt.

Hector began to tell him Garlic's history as far as it was known, taking care to make the tale relevant. By the time he had finished Clifford and Garlic shared the kind of affinity which can only exist between a boy and a battle-scarred cat.

"But only half of them came up, and half of those grew eight inches high and had no bloom and the other half flowered as soon as they emerged from the soil," Judith complained to Betty who had introduced the subject of bulbs.

"And you had put them in at the same time?" Betty enquired.

"Same bulbs. Same time. Father's never did anything like that. And he didn't fuss over his at all. Just plonked them in and forgot about them."

"Something to be said for just plonking things in," said Betty. "The more you fuss over them the more disappointed you are if they don't flourish."

"She's a great plonker, my Betty," Jim Redfearn explained, "but she has a touch of the green thumb too. Flowers right up to October. All summer, in spite of the heat, in spite of a small garden, flowers and more flowers. A blaze of colour."

"Well, it's because of all the digging you do," said Betty generously. "He makes the beds good and puts plenty of food in the soil," she added, and Judith, noticing with a spread of love deepening in her like a rich sunset that Hector was being nice to poor Clifford, exclaimed,

"Of course. Compost. Compost is the answer to everything."

"It's not a political thing," Joe was saying. "I used to think it was just political exploitation which created the sort of conditions that exist in my parish. But it's much more serious and harder to change than that. It is not just that there are the rich and the poor but that we all accept there should be the rich and the poor. Whatever the system, unless we also have a moral revolution, nothing will change. That's really why I joined the Church," he added, remembering.

Alan Judson assessed the young priest as he spoke, noticing that Susannah too was listening to him with wrapt attention. He observed the dark indentations under Joe's eyes, the worried lines on his brow, his tense, brisk gestures. He realised with a sense of compassion that there was a great gap yawning between what Joe was saying and what was going on in his mind.

"V..very difficult to achieve. And yet ess..essential," he agreed. "N..not a m..material problem. A moral one. A question of human g..generosity. Unless it arrives and prevails we're d..done for."

"Religion is a good start but you can't force religion on people and religion, too, goes wrong so often along the way." Joe wondered whether Alan had guessed.

"C..causes a f..few p..p..problems for us, religion. P..people pressing on r..ruthlessly against the natural flow of their own psy..psyches."

"Yes. I'm sure." Joe knew that he was being studied. "We have to find a balance, some way of giving ourselves entirely to others which fulfils us rather than squeezes us as dry as an old orange skin," he said guardedly.

There was a lull as all the conversations came to rest at once like a row of children on skateboards reaching the bottom of the hill and rolling slowly to a halt.

Judith smiled at the circle of her temporary family, turning her head to include them all and establishing that the sherry glasses were empty.

"Well," she said happily, "I think we might eat."

Susannah was already making her way to the kitchen to find out what she could do to help.

"Does Garlic eat now, as well?" Clifford asked.

Hector put his arm round the boy and the cat and whispering,

"Fish?" into Garlic's ear watched him uncurl himself and stroll towards the kitchen in Susannah's wake. He winked at Clifford.

"Uh-huh," he said.

63

"You can't judge everything by appearances. Just because I wear this collar doesn't mean that I'm your average, every-day, diligent parson."

He had been thinking for some time that he couldn't cope much longer with Susannah's snide comments.

"Just one of us agnostics at heart. Don't let Mrs Geraghty know. She'd be horrified to think that her host was being sanctified by a heathen." Susannah went on peeling carrots, slicing them, cutting them into small pieces and dropping them into a brown earthenware pot.

Joe could see that she didn't realise how serious he was, perhaps feeling that he had modestly underestimated his faith in order to make her comfortable. But she was comfortable already and took great delight in looking after his physical needs and even greater delight in undermining his already heavily undermined psychological landscape.

"Susannah. I wear this collar and I perform my priestly duties because I am an ordained minister of the Church. That does not mean that I am a pillar of the Church. It would be nice if you could realise that. Let up on the irony a bit. Go easy. Try to see things from my point of view."

"That's what I'm doing. You live in the midst of all this," Susannah enclosed the downtrodden parish with a wide sweep of the wooden spoon with which she had been tormenting the contents of the brown pot, "and you still have the nerve to go around talking about peace and goodwill and love."

He could murder her with the knife that was on the chopping board and go out and come back hours later to discover her body. Things like that happened in this area. It was the sort of end she might have met in the ordinary course of events if she hadn't been nicked for stealing babies and got on to her friend Hector's caseload.

He didn't have the energy to commit murder though, not even to prove a point to Susannah.

"If it's a theological debate you want I'm not in the mood," he said. "I'm going to write Sunday's sermon. If anybody phones or comes to the door I'm not in, unless it's urgent. And if it's urgent, it probably won't matter anyway."

Susannah understood that she had overdone it.

Joe was tired, that was all. He worked very hard. In fact, when she came to think about it, he worked harder than anyone she knew.

She grew thoughtful, adding a spliced leek to the vegetables and unwrapping a piece of meat to prepare it for the pot.

She had no feelings. At least, she had thought that she had no feelings. Josiah Harrison was not like any other man she had ever lived with. Normally she felt that she could say what she wanted to him. She could say what she liked without fearing that the whole establishment would go up in smoke. It had an air of indestructibility. Joe had an air of indestructibility. She could say what she liked. She could do what she liked. There was no way she was going to destroy Joe. He wasn't like the others, those whom she had watched becoming more and more insecure until they disintegrated under her scorn. Joe wasn't going to dissolve like an ice cube, leaving a muddy puddle in a footprint on the floor.

At least, she had thought that he wasn't.

She had taken on the job because it was all absolutely without emotional content.

She had thought that this was the significance of her presages of a journey, that this was why the big ship dogged her mind, the idea that she was going somewhere, towards a new shore which was untouched by her ferocious bitterness and her equally terrifying new experience of wanting to give herself. She had thought that during her time with Joe she might become one creature, of some sort or another. After all, this hallowed place was all that was hallowed in the environment of her childhood.

She had thought that Joe was absolutely safe from her because she had thought that Joe, too, was hallowed.

Then why did he mind what she said to him? Surely the thing about God was that He protected you from mere mortals, put you in to a state of invulnerability.

She gazed around the vast, echoing kitchen with its flagged floor. The flags were uneven and worn in hollows by generations of patient, submissive feet. There was something evocative about the flags. They reminded her that people were transitory, passed through places like water running through a ravine which alters so slightly, like the surface of the stone floor, that no matter how heavily or lightly or swiftly or slowly they proceed it is only after multitudes of them have tumbled away their lives that there is any evidence of their passing. She looked at the kitchen table. Its wooden top had been scrubbed into hollows like the flags. When she arrived at the vicarage it had been grey and neglected. She had cleaned it and bleached it until it was restored to its former white glory. How many good vicarage ladies had taken pride in this symbol of humble housecraft. She looked at the three bentwood chairs which she had stripped of their layers of paint, stained and polished and equipped with red cushions. They stood around the table like terriers begging for a treat. To the enormous cupboards which loomed like unassailable mountains along the entire wall she had added new coats of paint, as to restore them would have been a life's work. They, too, seemed to stand erect and solid with self-esteem, as though they could now shoulder whatever was required of them. She looked at the battle-scarred gas stove in which the pot was now beginning to simmer. She had come to understand its temperament and she would coax and wheedle it until it produced the satisfying smell of cooking. She looked at the rag-rugs which had been flat with years of grease until she washed them all in the gigantic Victorian bath and dried them under the trees in the autumn wind.

When she had replaced them they seemed to stretch themselves and lie luxuriant with colour like exotic birds sunning themselves in a firelight.

Suddenly she felt insecure.

She had become part of something established.

And Joe, apparently, didn't know whether he believed in its existence or not.

If God wasn't protecting him, she would destroy him. He would melt like all the others.

She knew, very clearly, that this was not what she wanted. Not any more. Once she had been jubilant when she destroyed somebody, something. Now she knew that she liked helping things to grow, supporting people. She had thought it would be a rest, living with Joe, not doing either, just drifting until she knew where she wanted to go, or found out at which port she had arrived.

She put two plates in the bottom of the old oven and two knives and forks on the cherished table top.

Then she walked very quietly to the scruffy room with its piles of books and papers and useful junk and armchairs which Joe glorified by the name of 'study'. She stood outside the door. After a few moments' hesitation she knocked, so softly that if Joe hadn't been sitting staring at a blank sheet of paper he wouldn't have heard her. On his face there was a look of despair as blank as the sheet of paper.

He jumped, as if the almost inaudible knock had been an assault on his body. He had become so used to living alone in this vault that it still took him by surprise to hear sounds of Susannah from its fastnesses.

"Susannah?" he called.

She opened the door and made her way across to the cluttered roll-top desk on which letters and bills and half-written articles and unwanted advertisements and ideas for sermons which had turned into nightmares had collected like a flock of swallows preparing to migrate to a better climate.

"Joe."

He looked at her and she could see that she had been right. He was desperate.

"Joe, I think I'll move on."

"You haven't been here all that long."

"No, but I think I'll go. Dad has asked me to go and live with him and Betty, to help with Clifford."

"As you wish. I've enjoyed your stay. Company, you know. Another body in the morgue."

"I'm not a body. I'm a person."

"As you wish," he said again.

She noticed that the page in front of him was blank.

"Sermon not going well?" she asked.

"What do you say?" Joe demanded. "What do you say to three Pakistani converts, an old man with a dog, four adolescent girls who have a crush on you and giggle throughout the service, and the redoubtable members of the Mothers' Union who swell the congregation week by week with great numbers of liberated children who wish to take over the Church?"

"And Mrs Geraghty," Susannah added.

"And Mrs Geraghty," he agreed. "Mrs Geraghty who believes that cleanliness is not next to Godliness but exceeds it as the Godhead exceeds the least of these her brethren."

There was a pause.

"You like people, don't you?" said Susannah.

"Yes, I like people. But the people I really want to talk to don't listen to me. And in any case, I have nothing to say. I don't know why I should be saying anything, or why anybody should be listening to me."

They stared at each other and in the dim light from the forty-watt bulb in the reading lamp they saw each other as insubstantial creatures. They heard the rain clattering on the tin-covered roof of the porch outside the front door, rattling in the leaves of the ivy which grew like a jungle on the vicarage walls.

There was another pause.

Between them, like a pool under trees as evening draws in, lay a whole eternity of weeping; frustrated, dry, harsh, grief-stricken weeping.

"Well, supper will be ready in about an hour," said

Susannah, moving towards the door. When she reached it she turned and looked back at the young priest.

She didn't know why it should happen just then, or why it should ever happen at all, but she realised that she was flying again. Her flying feelings descended upon her, better than in the administration of the anaesthetic before the ECT, better than in moments with Hector and Judith, better than they had at George's christening. She felt as if she were being drawn gently up into something that belonged to the whole of creation, a kind of consolation, a reality almost obscured by the greed and egotism and stupidity with which nations massacred each other. But the reality was always there, just beyond our understanding.

Something from herself was drawn into the vacant misery of Joe's eyes, as moisture is drawn up into the clouds by the sun.

She walked slowly back to the kitchen.

Perhaps the voyage was over. Certainly she knew that she now had a locker and a berth. She no longer felt particularly curious about the name or nature of the port in which she found herself.

But she decided that she wouldn't leave Joe, not just yet, anyway. She'd try to think of a nice way of telling him.

You never knew. It might cheer him up.

64

It seemed intolerable to Susannah that Joe should be allowed to suffer as he was suffering.

What could God be about, letting a good chap like Joe lose touch with Him while still expecting all the usual services? She was sure that He was there, somewhere there, with Father Wormold and the poor who were dead and that He was waiting for her and George. But was He enjoying this spectacle which distressed her so much? If people were anything to go by, He could well be. It depended on whether you felt that God was made in man's image or man in God's and if the latter, what God's image was. Either way, Joe had a raw deal, being left in the lurch like that.

"It's called the Dark Night of the Soul," Joe explained one evening. "It's a recognised state. It's a religious trial. At least, that's the theory. As far as I'm concerned, it's just a different viewpoint. Maybe the whole thing's an elaborate fiction. I've looked everywhere, tried everything. It all seems academic, not related to myself."

"You're just worn out," Susannah replied. "Your nervous system has had enough thinking and trying to pray and trying to find answers and work things out and bring light into darkness. How long is it since you had a holiday, I mean a proper holiday?" Susannah had never had a proper holiday but she had heard Hector saying things like this to people.

Joe couldn't remember. He had worked, at any job he could find, during his student vacations. Since then there had always been too much to do.

"I could go on a Retreat," he said doubtfully, "but I don't somehow think it would do a lot of good."

"I think you should stop trying," Susannah said decisively.

"The more you want something and the harder you try, the more impossible it becomes. If you forget about it for a bit, maybe it will happen."

In responding to these very profound deliberations Joe relaxed, and though God did not happen to him, Susannah did.

65

Having Susannah happen to him was no easier for Joe than everything else had been.

They lay, squashed together in his priestly single bed, wanting to make love, not knowing how to traverse the ground which lay between animus and anima, between body and soul; the body had let them both down on countless occasions, the soul to both of them appeared a contradictory, doubtful concept.

"I can't." Joe lay on his back.

"Why can't you?"

"It doesn't work any more. It hasn't for years."

"Rubbish," said Susannah. "You're young and fit. You're not impotent."

"It's a mortal sin."

"If I had been married to you in church I could have been married to you for your money, or for your handsome physique, or because I'd been made pregnant by somebody else, without having an ounce of love for you, without any passion. That would have been all right, for fifty or sixty years, carnal satisfaction?"

"It's the rules."

"Bugger the rules." Susannah had been listening carefully to the Voice of the Church for the past few weeks. "Your Jesus said that He had come to write the rules in our hearts. It's only that the rules have all been built up again over the centuries."

Joe was sweating.

Whatever had been fermenting, corked down for he knew not how long in the rigid container of his will, was bursting to be drunk, to be enjoyed, to be used as it had been meant to be used.

He looked at Susannah, unconcerned, sensible, wanting to love him. He looked at her brown limbs, her small, aware face, her smooth hair which now lapped over her thin shoulders as the water laps the worn furrows beside a brook, and he told himself that sex was not God.

Susannah turned on her side to face him, partly to make room on the sepulchral plinth.

"If the sin bit worries you too much, forget it," she said. "I mean, it isn't important. I don't want to be responsible for making you unhappier than you are already."

"No, it isn't that."

"What then?"

"I've done it all before. It's not the answer."

"So have I. There is no answer. It's all guesswork, trial and error." She wiped the sweat from his forehead with the corner of the pillowcase and nestled her head against his neck.

He held her, at first with a tense, frightened grip, as if she might suddenly slip away from him and be gone, lost through his indecision.

He relaxed a little, holding her more gently, knowing that she was here to stay.

Then peace began to descend on them and they lay absorbing each other's hurts and suffering which in turn became a new quality, a unique benison which they shared, which united them.

Susannah found that she could not equate this unison with anything that had ever happened to her. She knew that there was nothing to be said, that there would never be anything to say about it. It simply existed, a state which was undeniable though it could be denied, a state which they could either accept as their own particular, inexplicable, ultimate atonement or dismiss as an unfortunate lapse. She also knew that religion, Joe's specific religion, had both nothing and everything to do with it.

Joe had no such thoughts. He did not know at all what was

happening to him. This was not sex, this was a path which was leading him in the direction he wanted to go. Whereas before he had found that women beckoned him up promising, exciting cul-de-sacs, Susannah was simply here, Susannah was now.

Feeling Joe's body change Susannah began to respond; she was no longer in any doubt about her identity, her femininity. She had been looking for them in isolation, as if they should appear from nowhere as an oak tree, its seed carried by the wind, appears mysteriously in the middle of a field. They had, in fact, of course, been hidden in Joe. She responded as the sea responds to the breeze, as the streams respond to the sun, as everything elemental and human responds to what is elemental and human.

"Go on," she said when he hesitated. "Everything's all right. Go on."

Then she felt him inside the whole of herself, inside whatever constitutes the body, whatever constitutes the soul. They were flying, and they were flying together.

"Yes, yes, yes, yes, yes," Joe whispered, as if he had been affirming creation. He opened his arms to everything that he had shut out. His wilderness was about to explode into flower.

"Susannah," he said, "oh God."

Susannah laughed. And as when she had cried for Father Wormold it had not been because she was sad but because she was happy, so now she laughed for the sorrows of the world, for the neglected, the lonely, the starving, the imprisoned, for those who didn't have Joe. She laughed for her half-brother Clifford, for her dead mother, who had always been dead. She laughed because she knew that whatever God was, all of these people were His and that He would have the two of them, as one, in due course, as He had Father Wormold, as He would have George, as He had . . . Gavin?

Then she laughed because it was funny, and because Joe was laughing.

It was a beginning.

66

"Astonishing," said Hector.

They were having supper after coming home from the Christmas Fair at Josiah Harrison's church.

"Could you have believed it? Our savage little Susannah presiding as the first lady of the parish."

"I could," Judith replied. "Under the savagery there was always something selfless. It just needed a proper outlet."

"But who'd have thought it would find an outlet like that?"

Hector had doubts. He didn't want Susannah returning to his caseload a religious maniac in six months' time.

"L..L..Love." Alan spread a layer of marmalade on his bacon sandwich and began to eat it with energy and enjoyment.

"Why do you put marmalade on your bacon?" Hector enquired.

"I p..p..put marmalade on toast after eating bacon at b..breakfast," Alan explained. "It all g..goes down the same w..w..way. She's in l..love with him. In l..love with Joe," he added.

"That's like saying we should put custard on steak and kidney pie," Hector pointed out. He did not want to think about Susannah being in love with Joe.

"A l..l..lot of people d..do," said Alan. "And with g..good reason."

"And he's in love with her," Judith concluded comfortably. It seemed too fortunate to be true that after such a disastrous life Susannah should find someone to love who also loved her.

"Well, I don't know. I think possibly they are propping

each other up. They have complementary strengths and weaknesses," Hector suggested.

"That's what it's a..b..bout." Alan looked round the kitchen to see what was going to follow his bacon and marmalade.

"There's some ice-cream," Judith told him, "or cheese. Nice Camembert."

"Wish I'd known about the C..Camembert. It would have gone in my s..sandwich."

Hector watched Judith as she moved about, taking away the plates, bringing back the ice-cream and the cheese.

He remembered what he had done to her, what he had done to Susannah.

He supposed that by interfering in their lives he had harmed them both.

Yet Judith had survived and begun again, like a plant which survives the winter. And now Susannah was beginning to flourish. It seemed as if the real motives for living were indestructible, like the magnetism of the stars.

He sighed contentedly.

"How about rounding it off with an aperitif?" he asked Alan. "What would you like?"

"Anything. Anything will d..do."

"Tomato juice?" Hector suggested.

"N..N..Not tomato juice," said Alan firmly. "It wouldn't go with the marmalade."

67

Tessa looked adoringly at Susannah, sitting across from her at the little table, shuffling the grubby playing cards.

Around them the other patients talked in slow, sedated voices or chattered incoherently, beyond sedation, bulky, ruined forms of women who had been through too many storms, real or imaginary, who had retreated into the relatively safe waters of a degree of insanity, who had made the last plea for love and had it answered by the hospital authorities.

The Asian girl had been moved to Whittingham. There she would be living in ethereal silence like a Victorian pedlar doll under its glass dome surrounded by the intricate minutiae of her schizophrenia. But these women would be breathed on gently by the patience, the skill, the dedication of people like Hector and Alan and would be restored to their lives with a new assurance, to cope, as best they could, for the rest of their lives; or until it happened again.

Tessa had no idea who Susannah was. She had no recollection of the wild character with the butterfly hair-decoration who had bathed her so many centuries ago, at the beginning of the summer. She did know, however, that it was Wednesday, and that on Wednesday when she woke in the morning Nurse Ramsden would say,

"Come on, flower, rise and shine. It's Wednesday. Who comes to see us on a Wednesday?" and she would reply,

"Susannah, to play with me."

"You old bugger," Susannah exclaimed, "you've got some ingenious method of cheating. You beat me every time." And she dealt the cards, slapping them down on the red formica with all the apparent ease of a hardened gambler, though she was hopeless at cards and they bored her to distraction.

Tessa, however, did not.

Tessa was improving. No longer the malnourished creature who had been found, living alone, neglected and depressed, she had been helped and coaxed into a state in which she was almost ready to go to a sheltered housing scheme. She had been re-created, as an antique treasure is re-created by care and affection to a semblance of its former splendour.

"You look like me," said Tessa, approvingly.

"I'm a bobby-dazzler," Susannah agreed amiably. "I'll bet you were a bobby-dazzler, too."

"A right bobby-dazzler." Tessa offered Susannah a polo-mint and took one herself. "All the lads after me." Her face clouded and she added warningly, "But don't let 'em getcha."

"Never," said Susannah. "Never in this world."

"Ruin you. Love you and leave you." She spread the cards out in her old hands and examined them shrewdly. "Look what happened to me."

"I'm looking," said Susannah. "What happened?"

"Ruination. Thrown out. Disowned. From everything to nothing. Big do's and little do's. Never darken my doors. Father," Tessa explained obliquely.

"So you'd been a bad lass."

"Nature," Tessa said philosophically. "Nature, same as always. Catches up sometimes. Sometimes it don't."

"Caught up with you."

"Died at birth. Still wouldn't have me back. What would the neighbours say?" Tessa slapped her cards down and grinned triumphantly.

Susannah thought there must be something about this card game that was evading her.

She tried to imagine the mental attitude which would dispossess forever a daughter who was pregnant. No. It wasn't hard to imagine. Her father would have done it if Gavin had been in the offing while she still lived under his roof.

"So what then? Where did you live?"

"No place for a ruin in them days. People liked respectability. Most people. Not a question of money. Morals. Good living. Had to live good or couldn't find the wherewithal. No jobs with homes. Home job."

"You went into service. That was a come down."

"Tough titty," said Tessa ruminatively. "Only one as 'ould have me, the vicar. Worked for the vicar's family. Doing good, taking me on."

Susannah felt herself going red.

"Did you stay long, with the vicar, I mean?"

" 'Til I retired. Three vicars. Went with the vicarage."

Susannah felt a cold draught in her spirits, as if somebody had opened the front door into a cosy room on a rough night. She knew before she opened her mouth to ask the next question what the answer would be.

"St John's?" she said casually, as if Tessa had told her once before.

"It was a dump and hard graft. Weird folk, the clergy," Tessa continued as if Susannah had not spoken. "But better than the street."

Susannah had been scrubbing the flags, washing the rugs, painting and polishing the furniture once laboured over by Tessa.

It seemed obscene that she should have found celestial liberty within the same walls which had imprisoned her old friend.

68

"Hector," said Judith, "Hector, what's wrong with us all?"

Christmas and the New Year had passed, the memory of them fading with the falling of the snow. Deep and healing it soothed the moorland around the cottage, thick and grey in the darkness it sat on the windowsills far up the windows as though approving of the wholesome lethargy inside.

"What did you have in mind?" Now that the snow occupied the world and the garden was clothed with its blessing, Hector had taken to stoking the fire in the sitting room with the same enjoyment that he usually derived from trying to light his pipe. Every Saturday he collected logs from a farmer who was clearing his land. They were piled high on each side of the big, square fireplace. "I mean, what do you think is wrong with us, my dear?"

Only one small lamp illuminated the room but the flickering of the flames from the fire made moving shadows which gave an atmosphere of lulled comfort, as though the room itself were swinging gently like a cradle.

"Well, we can't live within our own surroundings. We have to go beyond our own emotions and tasks. We always have to look for something more, for something else."

Unlike lighting his pipe which was purely a personal pleasure, stoking the fire gave Hector the feeling that he was tending his homestead. He poked at a log which was about to fall on to the hearthstone.

"Uh-huh," he agreed.

Realising that if he poked at the log any further he was going to dislodge two other logs which were leaning against it he turned to the more predictable activity of lighting his pipe.

To his disappointment it lit the first time. He puffed at it rather sadly.

"Il faut cultiver son jardin," he mused, between puffs, "but the garden has now been enlarged to include the whole planet. The whole universe even. Our consciousness is being subjected to a constant stream of new ideas, new horrors, new possibilities. They hit us all day long, like a shower of meteors. It takes great strength, and some courage, to ward them off, or bother to sort through them for the valuable bits . . . minerals and so on."

He watched Judith as she stroked Garlic, draped over her knee on his back with his head hanging luxuriously bathed in the heat from the fire. Her hands were calm, expressing tenderness which the cat accepted with the regal grace of cats who know that it is due to them.

"It sometimes makes me feel very frightened."

Hector gave her a slightly wary look.

"You still feel frightened?" he asked.

"There's so much of everything. So many things can happen. Think what has happened to us. Think what has happened just in this house, in the sixty years we know about, to say nothing of the hundred years that went before." Judith's face, lit by the flames, turned from Garlic to her husband, seeking the reassurance that she knew she would find there.

"Stop the world you want to get off?" he suggested.

"Don't be silly, Hector. You know it's not that. It's just that we can't ever be sure of anything."

"We can't. You're right."

"Except that we are going to die."

"That's fairly certain, my dear."

"What else is there?" Judith stood up and Garlic grunted reproachfully as she unrolled him on to her chair. She chose a record from Hector's collection and switched on the record player. Then she lifted Garlic and spread him over her knees again like a woolly rug. A little trickle of woodsmoke crept out of the corner of the fireplace and wound its way into the lenient shadows as the music's harmonies filled the room. "I mean, Hector, what else is there?"

Hector allowed himself a moment of vulnerability.

"You and me?" he suggested.

"Yes, and everybody else. We are all you-and-me's. We can't confine ourselves to one you-and-me. We have to branch out. I don't mean just you, Hector. I'm not talking about Susannah. We need you-and-me's on a vast scale in order to give ourselves a feeling of certainty."

Hector discovered that his pipe had gone out. He fished in his jacket pocket for his matches and began to strike them and suck at his pipe with an expression of concentrated pleasure.

"Well, that's it then, Judith," he said between puffs. "If we can get that message across in the right places, we've cracked it. And for ourselves we have a strange assortment of people to make us certain of something, one of whom, judging by the noise outside, is about to enter with his customary vigour, stammer out an apology for having missed supper, and unwind himself in front of our fire."

"He hasn't missed it," Judith replied serenely. "It's in the oven waiting for him. We couldn't let him go hungry just because he forgot to be here."

And as Judith made her way through the firelight and the music and the scent of the burning wood to the kitchen and Alan fell through the front door with a flurry of snow, Hector confided in Garlic.

"I imagine that's another certainty," he said.